PEN

LEM

Kenule Beeson Saro-Wiwa was born in 1941 at Bori, on the southern coast of Nigeria. He was brought up in a large, supportive family with strong tribal links. He was educated at Government College, Umuahia, where he later taught, and at the University of Ibadan. In the mid 1960s he became a graduate assistant at the University of Nigeria, and then an assistant lecturer at the University of Lagos.

Saro-Wiwa's interest in politics emerged during the late 1960s, when he was appointed administrator for Bonny, Rivers State. He had spells as Commissioner for Works, Land and Transport; Education; and Information and Home Affairs. In the early 1980s he turned to writing, and in 1983 he published his first novel. His very successful television series, *Basi and Company*, ran from 1985 to 1990. His most highly respected work was *Sozaboy: A Novel in Rotten English*: an odd mixture of pidgin and idiomatic English, it is a satirical portrait of the corruption of Nigeria's military junta, with a bitingly humorous edge.

From 1990 his writing was ousted by his role as President of the Movement for the Survival of the Ogoni People (MOSOP), and he embarked on a campaign to bring their plight to the attention of the world. In 1993, after the election-day disturbances, Saro-Wiwa was imprisoned for a month and a day, an experience which is recounted in the poignant *A Month and a Day: A Detention Diary*, also published by Penguin. In May 1994 four Ogoni leaders were killed, suspected of collaborating with the military authorities, and Saro-Wiwa was again arrested, but this time the charge was murder – an accusation he always denied.

On 31 October 1995 Ken Saro-Wiwa was sentenced to death. Ten days later he was executed at Port Harcourt, Nigeria.

LEMONA'S TALE

KEN SARO-WIWA

PENGUIN BOOKS

PENGUIN BOOKS

Published by the Penguin Group
Penguin Books Ltd, 27 Wrights Lane, London w8 5TZ, England
Penguin Books USA Inc., 375 Hudson Street, New York, New York 10014, USA
Penguin Books Australia Ltd, Ringwood, Victoria, Australia
Penguin Books Canada Ltd, 10 Alcorn Avenue, Toronto, Ontario, Canada M4V 3B2
Penguin Books (NZ) Ltd, 182–190 Wairau Road, Auckland 10, New Zealand

Penguin Books Ltd, Registered Offices: Harmondsworth, Middlesex, England

First published in Penguin Books 1996
3 5 7 9 10 8 6 4 2

Typeset in 10/12pt Monotype Sabon by
Rowland Phototypesetting Ltd,
Bury St Edmunds, Suffolk
Printed in England by Clays Ltd, St Ives plc

CHAPTER ONE

Lemona

'Lemona. Lemona. Beautiful woman. Exquisite. She'll be hanged tomorrow. You know that, don't you? And you insist on seeing her? Well, I have no objection personally. But I don't know if she'll agree to see you. That's the problem. That woman is an enigma. In all my thirty years in service, I haven't met a prisoner like her. She doesn't talk to anyone, she's not had a personal visitor that I can remember. It's like she's not of this world. Even at her age, she remains very attractive. A beauty queen. I wish she could be saved. She shouldn't die. But she'll be hanged tomorrow at dawn. The warrant has finally been signed and delivered to me. It's tragic. A real tragedy.'

Thus, the Controller of Prisons at Port Harcourt prison, where I'd gone to request an interview with the condemned woman.

Not many will have remembered her, and her death would probably not affect many people. I was one of the few it ought to interest in a roundabout sort of way. And that is why I had arrived all the way from the United States of America, from San Francisco to be precise, to see her and interview her.

My guardian, whom I have not seen in years, has put me to it, and he won't tell me why until I have spoken to Lemona, he says. I would not have spoken to the woman ordinarily. I have enough of a burden to bear, visiting the empty, sad home of my murdered parents. And it's not as if I'm well-acquainted with home. I've been away for eighteen of the twenty-three years of my life. It's as though I could only return because my parents were no more. That they didn't want me in their life. Well, the pain of it is gone to some extent. It's two years since they passed away. And now, here I am to speak to the beauty who has been condemned to death for murdering my parents, although she denies it. Why should I speak to her?

'What you have not told me is what your relationship with Lemona is. You don't look like her, so you cannot be a daughter. You are not a journalist, are you? Right, you are not. A student. From the United States of America. We call this prison Alabama City. I don't know how it got the nickname, but Alabama City it is. And it holds at this time, one thousand and two hundred inmates, of which only thirty are women. Lemona is the most distinguished of them all. Distinguished by her demeanour and by her beauty. She's also the oldest of them. And she's, I repeat, an enigma. I'll let you see her, but I have to confirm with her that she'll be willing to see you. Wait a minute. I'll have to go and speak to her myself, otherwise she'll refuse flatly.'

He was gone, the balding, middle-aged, rotund man with a gap in his front teeth. He had bow legs, but was quite quick on his feet. He impressed me as a relaxed and helpful person, and it was thanks to his attitude that I felt like persisting in my task of seeing and interviewing Lemona. Had I met an obstacle in him, I would probably have turned back. The assignment does not excite me one bit.

In his absence, I surveyed his office. It was not as depressing as the prison itself. Indeed, it appeared neat and cheerful. And it must have been the only cheerful place in the entire establishment. The prison itself had shocked me from the moment I saw it. Grey, grimy and ugly, it looked most depressing from the outside. And the moment I crossed its iron gates into the building, I thought I was in, what shall I say, a dungeon. But that's not what I'm here for. Indeed, a lot had shocked me since my return. I had heard of the atrocious living conditions in the country in spite of its enormous wealth. But I did not begin to imagine how disastrous the situation was. Add to that the fact that I was being confronted, for some reason, with three connected deaths, and you will understand how nothing could really look attractive to me.

Maybe the only thing I was happy about was my guardian's house and the kind reception I had been offered there. It was as though he and his wife were out to make up to me for the turmoil in my soul they knew I would be experiencing. They installed me in a guest flat, set apart from the main house which, itself, was set in a spacious well-manicured garden in full flower with a riot of colours. And I had everything I wanted of creature comforts. The icing on the cake was that I didn't have to do anything for myself. There was a steward, cook, chauffeur, washerwoman, you name it. I was being spoiled. How sad that I could not really enjoy it all!

My guardian had a lot to tell me, apparently. He was the executor of my father's will. Since my arrival, I had not seen him. He had had to leave Port Harcourt in a hurry, but would be back in a week. He had, however, left instructions about my welfare and arranged for me to visit Port Harcourt prison to speak to Lemona.

'Sorry I took some time.' The Controller of Prisons was back. 'Lemona is an enigma. You know, she committed the first murder when she was twenty-five. And the other ones two years ago. She's fifty-two now, but looks thirty-nine, if a day. Ah, I shouldn't be telling you all this. The point is that dealing with her is not easy. There's no getting to her. She's put a deliberate concrete wall between her and the rest of the world. But when I told her there was a young woman who wanted to speak to her, her eyes lit up. She wants to know your name, how old you are and where you've come from. Then she'll let me know if she wants to see you.'

I supplied the pseudonym which my guardian had asked me to use while visiting the prison. My age and where I came from I could not hide. I had an unmistakable English accent, although there were now traces of an American drawl in it.

'Fine. I'll go and try again. I tell you, I'm only doing this as a service to a human being who is soon to die. What d'you call it? A humanitarian service. Yes? She's too sweet to be hanged. No. We should dispense with the death sentence. It's too cruel. But then, life probably has no meaning any more for Lemona. No meaning at all. I mean, she's been here for twenty-five years. And although prison has a life all its own, I wouldn't recommend it to my worst enemy. Understand? See you in a minute.'

*

He walked out of the room. I wondered if he would have been so forthcoming if he had known that I was the only daughter of the man and woman for whose murder Lemona had been condemned to death. It was just as well my guardian had suggested that I adopt a pseudonym. I sat and waited for what seemed like ages while all sorts of things crossed my mind. I imagined what Lemona would look like. I had not been aware that she had murdered someone else twenty-five years earlier. All I knew was that she had pleaded not guilty to the murder of my parents but had refused to testify in court. Nor would she allow an appeal to be filed on her behalf. The way I heard the story, she sounded like a nutcase. But the Controller of Prisons only thought she was an enigma. And he should know. He saw her quite often.

'Well, my dear Patricia (that was my pseudonym), you are in luck. Lemona will see you. But it will be some time. She's having to take a bath, and I guess she'll spruce up somewhat before she comes to see you. We can't deny her anything today, can we? I mean, it's her last day on earth. Terrible, isn't it? I wonder how I would feel if I knew that I had only a few more hours to live. You know, I've spent the last year hoping and praying that I would not be around when this lady was hanged. I've wished that I would be away on leave or on transfer when her papers arrived. But here I am; I'll have to supervise her hanging. My usual bad luck. I think I'm going to cry after the event. Like a baby. A baby. To be frank with you, I don't know why I feel this way. It can't be because she's so extraordinarily beautiful. No, although that may be one of the reasons. I think it's also because deep down in my heart, I think the world has been cruel to her, if she's not completely innocent. I can't imagine that anyone can be born as unlucky as she appears to have been. Well, maybe I shouldn't judge hastily. I don't have all the facts, if you ask me. All I have is what I've seen in the files. Someone should pry her story out of her. And that's why I'm happy you are here. I wish you were a journalist, you know. You'd have been able to put down her story for the rest of mankind. I hope, anyway, that she's willing to speak at some length to you. She's been quiet the last twenty-five years. I hope she can break the silence of a quarter of a century and pour her story out to you. I hope that's what you've come to do. Even if you didn't mean to, I mean, you should try and get her story. Do that for her, for us, for posterity, right?'

The Controller kept up this monologue as he sat in his seat opposite me. He did not look at me. Lost in his thoughts, he appeared to be expressing himself to the world. In another moment, he got up from his seat and began to pace about his office. He looked at his watch, and I followed suit. He paced the office in silence some more, hand on his chin, deeply thoughtful. I heard him sigh, and saw him shake his head, then look in my direction.

'One Controller lost his job here almost twenty years ago because of Lemona, you know. That was really some furore. I was newly employed then. I wasn't here, but the story rocked the prison service. The entire service. Every officer came to know about it. An official inquiry was set up and the Controller was dismissed. Dismissed. Lost his benefits. And he was a good officer, without as much as a query on his entire record. Pity. You know, as they say, God doesn't shut a door but he opens a window. Once out of the service, the man set up a private business. Today, he is a multimillionaire. He made it in twenty years. Made it big, real big. He's a big name hereabouts. Never forgave those who made him lose his job as Controller, I'm afraid. I blame him there. I mean, once God had been kind to him and given him money, he should have forgiven those who trespassed against him. But not this man. He wanted his pound of flesh, and went out to procure it long after everyone had forgotten that he still bore the hurt in his mind. He should have gone in with Lemona this second time, if you ask me. However, he has money, and was able to cover his tracks, leaving the poor woman to bear the brunt of the whole thing alone. All alone. He used her. Misused her. And she was his prey. So helpless, poor woman. It's not right. Not right.'

He stepped out of the office without a word to me. I turned round and instead of the Controller, I came face to face with a stately woman, tall and elegant, erect, with strands of grey, which gave her a distinguished look, in her hair. Her round face was calm, but there was sadness in her eyes. As a psychology student, I could read anguish in her eyes, although her face and total mien belied it. She was on the plump side, but it was easy to see that she would have been slim when she was younger. Although dressed in prison clothes, she still managed to look well-dressed. The very simplicity of the clothes enhanced her looks in a way that is difficult to describe. I thought of her as a queen. And a voice said to me, 'the queen of anguish'. The voice of the Controller of Prisons in my ear, I suppose.

All of the foregoing took place in a minute or so, as we looked at each other. I had thought that the Controller would come to introduce us, but he was nowhere around.

'You are Lemona,' I said, managing to force a smile.

'Yes. And you are Patricia.'

'Shall we sit down some place?'

She walked to the Controller's seat and sat on it, to my surprise. I took the seat I had been occupying directly opposite the Controller, across the table. I had my hands on the table and I noticed that Lemona stared steadily at my left hand. This made me a bit self-conscious, because part of my little finger is missing. I was teased a lot about it when I was very young. Lemona must have noticed it, because when I drew back my hand and placed it on my lap, she seemed to let her lip flutter in what might have been a smile. She then fell to staring me in the face. She seemed to be scrutinizing me. I returned the compliment. I thought I should remember for all time the murderess of my parents. There was emotion in her face as she looked at me. Then her gaze went past me to the door in front of her, as if she was trying to remember something.

I have never thought of myself as a pretty woman. I look very much like my father, I was always told, ebony black, with a flat, small nose and bright eyes. I felt uncomfortable under the gaze of Lemona, as an ugly woman will feel when placed side by side with a beauty queen.

The moments passed uncomfortably. I had to do something to break the ice that was slowly building between us. After all, I was the one who had requested to see her. I didn't quite know how to start, and made one false start after another, hiding my embarrassment in a little cough. While I laboured at it, Lemona said in a soft voice, mellow as honey, 'You asked to see me.'

'Yes,' I replied.

'Here I am.'

'I'm sorry if my coming is some trouble to you. I'm a research student at an American university. I heard about you and thought your story rather interesting, and I wanted to know a bit more about it. I hope you do not mind?'

'No, not at all.'

The bit about my being a research student at an American university was right. I had left Nigeria when I was five, being sent to a nanny in England who took care of me until I had done my school examinations at sixteen, before I was shunted to America, where I obtained a first degree in the humanities. I was now pursuing a graduate programme in psychology.

There is a bit of a story behind me, of course. All the time I was in England I got to see my father only during his annual leave, when he came to stay with me and my nanny in our Brighton home. I did not ever see my mother; she did not travel with him. He always told me that she was feeling poorly and had doctor's orders not to travel. When finally I got sent to America, I did not see my father again until he died. I continued to receive his letters, but he did say that he was unable for certain unspecified reasons to travel.

I did wonder why I was not being invited home to visit my parents, and that gave me a deal of worry. But I was not in a position to question my father. I depended entirely on him, and relied on his good sense. He was a Justice of the Supreme Court of Nigeria, I knew, and one of the best in the country, I was always told. My mother was also a Judge of the High Court. These were parents of whom I could be justifiably proud. And I expected that they would be proud of me too. Unfortunately for me, there seemed to be a dark shadow between us, which only my parents knew about. I had photographs of me and my dad in various places in England – on the beach in Brighton, at London Zoo, at various playgrounds, and in the house with my nanny. I had no pictures of me and my mother. I carried only one picture of my parents – their wedding picture.

I thought of this as I sat before Lemona, the woman who was

to die the following morning, less than twenty-four hours away. The Controller had said that she had a story behind her. I had to remember that I, too, had a story behind me. Everyone has a story, some dark, some bright. Lemona's story might well have crossed with mine at some stage. Perhaps that is what I was here to hear.

When Lemona spoke, there was a change in her voice, a more friendly touch to her tone, and I thought, though I may have been wrong, that there was a motherly hint in it too.

'I'm happy you found something interesting in my story. And all that way over in America. It's a story I've never told, because its owner was expected and had not yet come. I didn't think it worth telling to anyone else. But tomorrow is a special day and since you are here and express interest in it, daughter (may I call you daughter?), it must now be told. Hopefully, it may help other women find their way through life and help them to avoid the errors I made. It may not be very interesting, but it probably has some lessons. Are you ready to hear me out?'

'Yes.'

'It may take a very long time.'

'I have all the time in the world on my hands.'

'Ah.'

And she narrated the story which you are about to hear. I shall record it as I heard and memorized it. The tone of voice may be hers and it may be mine; it does not matter. As she narrated the story, I increasingly felt it to be mine, and I adopted it as such. But is not that the point of every story, especially a good story? That it strikes a chord in us, we recognize its intrinsic quality and relate it to our lives, our experience, and we adopt it, it becomes a part of us, a general experience, and goes into lore and becomes common property?

CHAPTER TWO

I was born to a mother who was the only daughter of her parents. She never did marry, it being the custom of our land not to give out the first daughter in marriage, she being encouraged to remain in her father's house and produce children for the family. I did not know my natural father, and my maternal grandfather having died while I was still young, I grew up in the care of my mother alone.

Ours was a little village, Dukana, in the back of the woods, the middle of nowhere. I recall it now, a small community of farmers and fishermen, where everyone knew the other. My mother was a farmer, taking care of one or two patches of farmland from the beginning of the year to the end of it. She was poor, and we barely had enough to live on from day to day.

We lived in a mud house, roofed with thatch, and there was not much in it. Clothes were whatever we could find to cover our bodies, and food was foofoo with a little broth, which might contain fish or periwinkles, or not. Ours was a hard life, our lot a difficult one.

In spite of this, I had a happy childhood, my situation being no worse than that of those with whom I played on the sands of the village, with whom I danced or told folktales by the fire or in the moonlight. As a girl, I did all those things girls of my age did, fetching water early in the morning from the stream, helping my mother to cook, fetching firewood from the farm or the forest and returning home with a little bundle neatly balanced on my head, and going to the early-morning or late-evening market to buy food or fish.

My happiest memories are of the festivals of Dukana, the first being held at the beginning of the year, when the planting season began. Little girls were a very important part of this festival, and we would prepare for it by practising dance steps at night for several weeks. And when the dances and songs were perfect, we would appear in public, our bodies painted with henna, our hair coiffed in neat plaits, with heavy beads around our waists, our necks and our ankles. Our parents would watch us as we moved from one compound of the village to the other, our mothers ululating, fathers and uncles offering us gifts of yams because we had danced or sung well.

Although I had no father and my mother was all alone, this early yam festival always fetched me a lot of gifts, for reasons which I could not tell, and I think my mother looked forward every year to it because it gave me so much joy, and fetched us a lot of yams, with which my mother planted her farm patches.

Later in the year, during the harvest, there would be another festival, the New Yam Festival, at which we celebrated the fruit of the land and our labour for the year. Food was the theme of the festivities, and we would cook our best meal that day, offering friends and family what we were able to produce from the land. On the day, we would ensure that we had the biggest fish, and that our meal was prepared with care and attention. On this day, the young boys made camouflage out of a particular climbing plant, so that they looked like moving bushes. The girls would tease them, and they would come after us, and we would disappear into our houses. Then our parents would emerge from the houses and offer the masqueraders gifts of yams.

Two or three months later would follow the Annual Festival, in which the village celebrated the passing of another year. Again, it was a time of dancing and eating, of fêting friends and family.

And then, finally, would come the period of Christmas and what was termed the White Man's New Year, a week during which we wore new clothes and went to church, most people in Dukana professing the Christian faith. We hung palm fronds in front of our houses shortly before Christmas and on New Year's Eve, at midnight, the adults would take them down, and with cries of 'Year out' and 'Away with all evil', they would sing and dance to the waterfront and throw the fronds into the creeks.

And that would signal to us children that the planting season was nigh.

It was a simple, joyful life which I took part in and enjoyed along with my friends. No matter the situation of my mother, I did not feel a sense of loss or of inadequacy. We were a part of the community, playing our role, and as I say, there was not much difference between me and my friends, as far as I could tell.

There was a school in Dukana, which children were expected to attend if their parents could afford it. And this is where the difference in our upbringing began. My mother was all alone, but she wanted me to do what other children did. And so, when I was old enough to go to school, she made sure I went there. I believe that even at that time, it was recognized by all that the school was the way to a happy future. Because we did notice that our teachers lived better than others. They were the ones who rode bicycles, and lived in slightly different houses. They were the ones to whom others looked up, and they were the ones who were seen or thought to be close to the new wisdom which brought the things we never had in Dukana, but which could transform our lives for the better.

I liked it at school, playing with my friends and learning to read and write. All I needed for a start was a square slate and a hard pencil, or a little blackboard made of plank and painted so that chalk would show up on it. That and new clothes to wear, since there was a school uniform.

In the beginning, my mother could not afford a uniform, and she spoke to the teacher to allow me to go in my home clothes until she could provide me with a uniform. He agreed, but it made me feel different from all the other children, and I did not like it. I cried every day after school, and badgered my mother until, miraculously, the school uniform arrived. I used it throughout the week and mother would wash it over the weekend and get it ready again for the next week.

One reason I liked school was that it freed me from going to the farmland with my mother every day. Once I had begun schooling, I only went there on Saturdays. Sunday was reserved for church and Sunday school, where we learnt about Jesus Christ and how he gave his life to save the world.

For the first few years, when the fees were not very high, my mother could afford to keep me at school, and I learnt among other things to speak English, from the third year of schooling.

But it became increasingly difficult for her to meet the requirements of school fees, books and uniform as I grew older, and after some time, I dropped out of school.

That was, certainly, the most painful experience of my young life, and it may have been the begetter of the string of disappointments I was to have later in life. It hurt me a lot at that time, as much in the way it happened, as in the happening.

I wish my mother had called me and told me I would not be returning to school after the holidays because she could no longer afford to keep me in school. She did not do that, maybe because she could not bear to give me the bad news herself. She allowed me to return to school and then, as was usual, after three weeks, the names of all those who had not paid their fees were read out, and we were all asked to leave the class.

This happened to me every beginning of term, and I would go home and lay siege to my mother with tears and more tears. I would refuse to eat, to do housework, and would so harass my mother that in the end, she would rather get me back to school than suffer the harassment I was giving her.

One incident of that period of my life sticks indelibly in my memory. A group of us, girls, had gone to the stream to fetch water for our teachers and for the school. We each had a clay pot which we used in those days for fetching and storing water. As usual, we spent time bathing and splashing about in the cooling stream. We played about quite a lot too before we would finally fill the pots and return to school.

On that particular day, I found in my attempt to fetch water that my pot had been broken, a gaping hole at its bottom. I was in distress. I knew that I had not hit the pot against anything and was not responsible for the hole. Who had done it? All the girls denied responsibility for it. But, surely, one of us had done it while running past the row of pots.

Disconsolate, I trudged back to school behind the other girls, who had their pots finely balanced on their heads. When we got back, our teacher immediately noticed that I was carrying an empty pot. I explained what had happened, denying that the fault was mine. The teacher asked around, and everyone denied responsibility. Whereupon, he decided that I was to blame. He asked for an explanation. I refused to say a further word. He gave me six strokes of the cane on my hand for being careless. I held myself and refused to cry although I was hurting badly. And all that day at school, I refused to say a word to anyone. I would not answer questions in class, and there was not a tear in my eye.

The story eventually got to my mother, and she questioned me as to what had happened. I refused to answer her questions and maintained a stolid silence thereafter. No amount of cajoling or threats would make me budge. For good measure, I refused to eat my meals for a whole day and refused to return to school for a whole week thereafter. I only relented when I noticed that my poor mother was going almost berserk with worry. I returned to school, and no one ever referred to the incident of the broken pot again.

My time at school was not to end at the most senior class. My mother could not afford to send me to school any more. The burden had become too great for her and I had, much against my wish, to drop out. The pain of it burnt and scared my very soul, as I saw my friends go every day to school while I pottered around Dukana, going with my mother to the wretched patch of land where she planted yams, cassava and vegetables, and did menial chores around the house from day to day.

Even at that time, I had begun to harbour certain ambitions, lowly no doubt, but ambitions all the same. We spoke of it at school. I thought of becoming a nurse some day, of wearing that beautiful white uniform I had seen when a nurse came to the school to inoculate us against smallpox. I admired her so, I spent days and nights wanting to be like her. I dreamt, oh how much I dreamt. And from then on, school became very important to me. Thus the abrupt end of my school-days proved the end of my first dream.

I must have been one of the unhappiest beings in the village that year. My mother did all she could to cheer me up, but I was disconsolate. The realization that I had no way out of my situation frustrated me even more. Yet, looking at my mother's helplessness, I knew I could not blame her for it. She had done all that was within her power for me and would have done more were she in a position to do so.

I cast my mind back now, as I have done these many years, and I think of her, illiterate, without a husband, a father or any useful relatives, without money, and wonder why she had to be like that. What did life really hold for her? And I have concluded that maybe I was the only life she had. I was her only hope, the only reason she could go on living from day to day. Her utter helplessness, the wretchedness of her life, has now dawned on me. And yet, I ask, was she not better off than me? Was she not? At least she had her freedom to go and come, and I have not managed to have even that. And she did not end her life as I am going to end mine tomorrow. But I digress.

One day, I was at home, when the headmaster of the school I had just dropped out of came to our house to speak to my mother. I was just going to the stream when he called. Upon my return, my mother called me.

'Lemma,' she said, 'would you like to leave Dukana?'

'Why?'

'You saw the headmaster of your school talking to me when you were going to the stream. He came to ask if I would allow you to go and stay with someone in the township.'

I was beside myself with joy. The boredom of staying in Dukana was getting under my skin. Anything to relieve it was most welcome. I jumped at the opportunity.

'Who am I going to stay with?' I asked.

'I don't know him,' Mother replied, 'but if it's all right by you, I will tell the headmaster and the man will come to collect you.'

'Why?'

'I don't know,' my mother answered.

One week passed. A long week, during which I spent my time dreaming of life in a township. A place with big storehouses and cars, where there were lights day and night, where there were a lot of nurses in hospitals, all dressed in white. I dreamt of a wonderful life, beyond anything I had ever imagined.

So when my master finally turned up in a car, I was more than ready to jump into the vehicle and leave on the instant. My little bundle containing a few clothes had been ready for a whole week, waiting only to be grabbed at short notice. I did not look at the man who was taking me away. I knew nothing about him. I did not know where he was taking me to. All I knew was that I would be away from the boredom that was Dukana, the tedium that was my daily life, away from school, from my mother's house. I did not even ask Mother whether there were any terms under which I was leaving.

I suppose Mother was happy to let me go. She had probably wondered what else she could do for me. And she would most likely have come up with the answer 'Nothing'. Beyond waiting for the years to roll by, and as I now realize, marry me off to a man, any man, probably the first man, who came to ask for my hand in marriage. And she would receive a sum of money which would last her no more than a few months, after buying herself one or two new blouses and sarongs.

I wonder now, as I have wondered over the years, if she thought at all about what she was letting me in for. Or did she trust the headmaster of the school so absolutely? Anyway, that day, as I headed for the car, she hugged me and cried gently.

'Go well, my daughter, my beautiful Lemma, my only daughter. Behave well and you will be happy. The man will send you to school after some time.'

This was the only inkling I had that my departure for the township might alter my condition beyond easing the tedium of my life. As I got into the car and was driven off, I waved my mother goodbye. I saw her stand, a thin figure, in clean but worn, almost tattered, clothes, her hand in the air, waving me goodbye, a burden taken off her weary shoulders.

In no time we had left the rickety, rural houses of Dukana far behind, and the bushes and the road were flashing past us at dizzying speed. It was a completely new experience for me. I had not ridden in a car all my life, not even on a bicycle, and I was all excitement, not only about the car, but about the new places through which we were passing; places I had only heard about, had never seen.

Sitting in the front of the car with my, what shall I call him, master, he did not speak much to me. 'What is your name?' he asked after he had driven out of Dukana.

'Lemma,' I replied.

He repeated the name after me, tried to pronounce it as I did, but was unable to. I knew then that he did not come from our area.

'How old are you?' he asked.

I did not know and said so.

'Did you finish your primary-school education?'

'No,' I replied.

I returned to my excited thoughts, and he drove on. I soon fell asleep and did not wake up until the car drew to a stop. I opened my eyes. Night had fallen. We were in front of a very big house (so it seemed extraordinarily big at the time), all ablaze with electricity. I was confused, dazed. I might as well have been in a trance. The man opened the car door for me and I tumbled out, my hand upon the little bundle of clothes I had brought along.

A woman came out of the house, embraced the man and beckoned to me to follow her.

'What's your name?' she asked.

'Lemma,' I replied.

'Welcome, my dear child. My name is Mrs Mana. The gentleman who brought you is Mr Mana, my husband. You will call me Mrs Mana, and he is Mr Mana. You understand?'

'Yes, Madam.'

'Not "Yes, Madam," but "Yes, Mrs Mana."'

'Yes, Mrs Mana.'

'Good.'

She led me through a large, well-furnished parlour to a room with one large bed and a small one. She indicated that the small bed was mine. The large bed was already occupied by two children, who were fast asleep.

'These here are my children. The elder one is Sarah and the younger one Paulina. You will get to know them tomorrow when they are awake. Keep your little bundle in your bed. Come and join me in the kitchen. You must be hungry.'

I did as I was told, and we moved into her kitchen. It was ever so different from what I was used to in Dukana! It took me quite some time to absorb it. It was all like a dream. A beautiful dream.

I did all I was told painstakingly. Mrs Mana was a good teacher. She did not assume that I knew anything. She taught me everything patiently, attentively.

That night, I learnt to lay the table for the couple and to serve dinner. After dinner, I did the dishes and put them away carefully before I had my own dinner in the kitchen. Then Mrs Mana saw me to the children's room. She examined my little bundle, went into her room and got me a nightgown – an old one that she probably no longer needed. And for the first time I slept in a nightgown.

CHAPTER THREE

The Nanny

I fell into deep and blissful sleep as soon as I lay in bed – the only comfortable bed in which I had slept in my life. That night, I had a horrible dream. I had gone into the forest with my friends to fetch firewood, as was our habit in Dukana. Somehow, I wandered away from the group and went deeper and deeper into the forest, where I chanced upon a most beautiful mansion laid in a lovely garden, its doors wide open. I cautiously moved into the house, attracted by its grandeur, and found it empty. I explored the house, passing from room to room, until I met a hideous monster in one of the bedrooms. As the monster tried to grab me, I screamed and turned and ran out of the mansion, back into a jungle so thick that I could not see in front of me. I called to my friends for help only to discover that they were no longer around. The jungle suddenly sprang several lions, slouching towards me, their fangs sending the jitters through my entrails. Lost and frightened, I screamed and screamed, and was still screaming when I opened my eyes, relieved to find it was only a dream.

My surroundings were clearly unfamiliar, and it took me some time to remember that I was no longer in Dukana in my mother's house. I stretched and yawned and was met with two quibish giggles. By the electric light I saw Sarah and Paulina, the two daughters of my employers, already awake and seated on their beds. They appeared to have been watching me. As I lay on the bed, Sarah, the elder one, came to me and asked, 'What is your name?'

'Lemma,' I replied.

'You are the new nanny?'

'Yes,' I answered. I did not understand the meaning of 'nanny'.

'You won't go away after a month as Iquo did?'

'No, she won't,' answered Paulina, the younger of the two.

'Iquo used to plait our hair every Sunday. She should not have left us,' Sarah complained to me.

'She should. Mummy spoke to her very harshly all the time,' Paulina asserted innocently.

'She was lazy, so Mummy said. She slept all the time and did not keep the house clean.'

'And she could not get us dressed for school on time,' laughed Paulina.

'She used to pinch my ear too.'

'She was very naughty,' Sarah added.

'More naughty than Ije, who came before her.'

The girls kept up a steady, innocent banter until their mother's voice floated into the room. 'Girls, are you awake? It's time for a bath.' She came into the room.

'Good morning, Ma,' I greeted.

'No. "Good morning, Mrs Mana,"' the two girls said in unison, and laughed.

'Come on, Lemona. You have to help bathe the girls and get them dressed, ready for school, then prepare their breakfast, make sure they eat and see them off to school. I'll show you how today.'

The girls trooped off to the bathroom. Mrs Mana put me through my paces by actually putting me to work immediately while she supervised me. Bathing and dressing the children was easy, but the breakfast they were to have proved strange to me. I knew nothing about cornflakes, fresh milk, nor did I know quite how to prepare stew. For us, in our home in Dukana, all meals were foofoo and broth. However, I think I learnt fast, and was soon preparing all the children's meals.

That first day, Mrs Mana walked with us to school and then came back to leave me instructions on how to clean the house. She went through all of it with me. I noticed that Mr Mana was not in the house. He had left even before the children began their breakfast.

Mrs Mana was very kind to me. She noticed that I did not have shoes on my feet as we prepared to walk the children to school. She gave me a pair of rubber slippers. 'Keep them,' she said. And, observing that I was almost the same size as herself, she gave me two of her old dresses, along with slips. 'I'll get you pants from the shop later today. You won't be using my old pants,' she said.

We went together to get the children from school at noon and had given them their lunch, when Mrs Mana went upstairs, got dressed (I found she was, of all things, a nursing sister) and drove off in the car in which we had travelled the previous day. She returned late in the evening. The children were playing with me in the parlour, and she hurriedly sent them to bed after ensuring that they had had their dinner.

Thus was my introduction to the Mana household. I was to come to learn that the house in which we lived was in the Government Reservation Area, an estate meant for top civil servants and business executives. Mr Mana himself worked in the Forex Drilling Company, and was involved in the search for oil which was going on at the time. He spent three weeks out on the rig and one week at home every month.

The house was a beautiful three-bedroomed bungalow, well-furnished and set in a garden with manicured lawns containing evergreen and fruit trees, very much like all the houses in the estate, some of which were, however, two-storey buildings.

The household was a happy one. Mrs Mana was efficient and extremely hard-working. Her standards of cleanliness were very high. But she was very quick-tempered and, I should say, intolerant of anyone who did not meet or rise to them. She was a pretty woman, round-faced, well-shaped, with what I came to know much later as a figure eight, and with a wealth of hair on her head. Her eyes were rather small and her neck long and shapely. She had a very expressive face, and her anger showed easily on her scornful lips. In her worst moods, she could be quite terrifying. But she was, until she was offended, a very pleasant person. She chatted gaily with her children, discussing with them as if they were her friends, which explained the way the children knew about things which were beyond their ages of seven and five. She was on the short side and I was already, at my age, the same height as her, if not slightly taller. And I was not yet thirteen.

Mr Mana, on the other hand, was a slim, gangly fellow, standing almost six foot tall, with lazy eyes, large hands and feet. He slouched around idly, in a manner at one with his gait. He spoke slowly too, when he spoke at all, for he was a very taciturn man. I did not see him play often with his children, and being at work most of the time, he tended to be far away from them. He seemed content to let his wife do everything around the house, giving orders and being bossy. He was almost always dressed in a light-cotton, short-sleeved shirt flying over a pair of trousers. He wore sandals all the time on his big feet. He was by no means a handsome man. In my early days in the household, I was very shy of him, and could not look into his eyes.

As I say, it was a happy household, the children being particularly responsible for the fun, laughter and sunshine which spread like ripples on the surface of water.

Thanks to the great assistance and insistence of Mrs Mana, who spared no pain in introducing me to the ways of the family and of modern living, I soon fitted into the family routine. She encouraged me a lot, did Mrs Mana. She would say, 'You're a very beautiful girl, Lemma. You'll grow to be a beauty queen. You must take care of yourself. You learn fast too, which is good. And you're a hard worker. Your mother must be very proud of you.' She always spoke to me in good English, even though I replied in pidgin English. Gradually, she and Sarah and Paulina made me learn to speak good English, even if haltingly at first.

I did a lot of household chores too, for I was the only helper in a big house. I could understand why the likes of Iquo and Ije did not last as house-helps. The size of the house made the work very demanding, and since Mrs Mana insisted on her own standards of cleanliness being maintained, a house-help had to be not only hard-working but single-minded and dedicated. A girl who had alternatives would not have stuck it for more than a month unless she was being paid enormous sums of money.

Unhappily for me, I did not have alternatives, or I had not found them. In any case, I was very innocent, having known nothing better than what I was going through. I was quite content with being away from the boredom of life in Dukana, and pleased that I had clothes to wear, shoes on my feet, three meals a day and a comfortable bed to lie in. Mother had mentioned briefly that I might be sent to school and, although I thought of it, I dared not ask. In any case, I was not in a hurry. I often took the children's books to read on those occasions when I found a moment to spare. However, such occasions were rare since my day was fully occupied, taking the children to and from school, cooking, cleaning and serving food.

When I arrived at the Mana household, I had not experienced my monthly pain. I had been there for a year and more when I finally had it. I seemed to be growing fast into womanhood, although I was still a teenager. I rose quickly above Mrs Mana and had to have a complete change of wardrobe. I noticed the physical changes in my body when I looked into the mirror. I was not only growing very tall, my breasts were growing bigger and firmer. They shot upright, so to say, and looked most inviting. Whenever I went out to have my hair done, which Mrs Mana permitted once a month, the women who did the plaits and braids remarked upon my attributes, which made me very shy. One was entirely taken up with the dimples on my cheeks, which I had not even noticed. Another remarked upon the straightness of my legs and the hair on my head, the firmness of my buttocks. Oh, the things they noticed, these women hairdressers of the market-place.

For the whole time I was in the Mana household, I had not been paid. However, all my requirements were met, and promptly too. So I did not have anything to complain about. Occasionally, my mind would flip to my mother and to Dukana. But that was only on occasion, particularly when Mrs Mana spoke harshly to me and reminded me that I came from the 'bush'. But such occasions were few and far between. Sometimes, also, Sarah and Paulina, in their innocent, childish chatter would remind me of my mother.

'Lemma, where's your mummy?'

'She's in the village.'

'Do you like her?'

'Yes.'

'Did she smack you when you were a little girl?'

'No.'

'Why doesn't she come here to stay with us?' Paulina would ask.

'Because there's no room, silly,' Sarah would reply.

'She could sleep on our bed.'

'And where would we sleep?'

'Can we go and see your mummy one day?'

'I'll ask Mrs Mana. For now, it's breakfast, and then school for you two.'

No, Dukana was far away. So also Mother. I was savouring the joys of township life. For all that, I did not go out much, since my duty lay in taking care of Sarah and Paulina, helping in the household chores – cleaning, washing, ironing and cooking. On occasion, whenever Mrs Mana went out with the children, she would take me with her, and again I recall how our hostesses would openly remark on my beauty and elegance, which remarks never failed to make me blush. Once or twice, I went with the couple and the children to Port Harcourt Club and was, I think, the object of a number of amorous looks and whistles. The club was another world altogether, with its swimming pool, tennis court, bar and restaurant.

Since that period of my life ended, I have realized that I was no more than a slave. For all that labour, I was not paid. I was only expected to be grateful that I was being fed and given clothes and shelter. There was the possibility of my being sent to complete my primary education and being taught a trade. This was broached from time to time, but I believe it was a way of keeping me quiet and contented so that I could continue to take proper care of Sarah and Paulina as they pursued their education. I was manna to the Manas. Mr and Mrs could pursue their careers knowing that their children were in safe, good hands. What happened to the hands did not particularly matter. Or did it?

Mr Mana always spent his week off in the month with the family in Port Harcourt. He normally arrived completely exhausted by the three weeks on the rig and would spend the time recuperating or catching up on family affairs that had accumulated during his three-week absence. He gave time to his wife, too; she would have made him do so, even if he did not want to. She never tired of letting him know that she was no mere housekeeper, meant to keep his house spick and span for his pleasure when he returned

23

from his home on the rig. Nor was she merely the mother of his children, fulfilling reproductive functions. He was lucky that she was willing to wait for him three out of four weeks every month. And he had better start thinking of other ways of keeping the family close. The children were growing and needed their father. She was not going to be a single mother. Thus, and more. Often in my hearing, although I was not meant to hear what was being said. Mr Mana would always plead gently that he was doing his best, had always done his best, would try to do even better in the future. The job was paying well, the extra allowances which came from being on the rig were very helpful to the finances of the family.

I had been a part of the household for more than two and a half years when the problem that was to send me away from the Manas began. I was always shy before Mr Mana. He was, after all, master of the house, and if Mrs Mana was far away above me and I dared not answer her back no matter what she said, Mr Mana himself was up in the high heavens, a god, as it were. He never spoke to me, beyond requesting me to fetch him his slippers, a towel or whatever, or asking me to do something for either Paulina or Sarah. He kept a studied distance from me. At first, I took all that for granted. Our relationship was that of master and servant and I understood that.

But on one of his days off from the rig, he had himself chosen to walk the children to school. Mrs Mana had taken the car to work and I was alone in the house doing the general cleaning as usual. When Mr Mana returned, I had completed my chores, had my bath and changed into clean clothes. Normally, I would have sat back in the parlour to listen to the radio or to play music on the radiogram. I always did that when I was alone at home, the children gone to school and Mr and Mrs Mana at work. Or else, I would go out to visit a nanny I had come to know next door.

But that day, Mr Mana being around, I remained in my room, and was looking leisurely through one of the children's books, another pastime I often indulged in, and from which I derived much satisfaction. I knew that the car being away, Mr Mana would return home after leaving the children at school. I was reading when the doorbell rang. I went to answer it and opened the door to let Mr Mana in. I welcomed him back and returned to my room.

I was leafing through the book I had been reading when I heard my name. 'Lemma!' It was Mr Mana calling.

'Yes, Uncle.' I could never call him Mr Mana although Mrs Mana had suggested that I do so. I only referred to him as Mr Mana if I was speaking to Mrs Mana. When I spoke to the children, I referred to him as 'Daddy'.

'Come here,' he ordered in a loud voice.

My heart missed a beat. Had I done something wrong? I went in search of him.

'I'm in the bedroom!' he called aloud.

I stood before the bedroom door and knocked timidly.

'Come right in.'

I opened the door, peeped in and entered with some trepidation. I noticed that he was in his nightshirt, the sort he always wore at bedtime. He was lying on his bed, reading. The air-conditioner was humming in the wall. I stood near the door. He got up from his bed, walked towards me, and shoving me gently aside, turned the key in the lock. Then he passed his arm around me, and drew me towards the bed. I was frightened as he pushed me gently into bed. I began to scream.

'Don't shout,' he urged me. 'I'm not going to hurt you. I promise, I won't hurt you.'

He began to stroke my hair with his left hand while his right hand cupped my left breast. I screamed and he stopped my screams by placing his lips on mine. I experienced a new sensation. No one had ever placed his or her lips on mine. I struggled to free myself from him, but he was powerful. He held me down with his right hand while the left pushed up my dress, then moved up my waist and began to pull down my panties. His lips were still on mine and I felt his tongue in my mouth. Once he had got my panties from my waist, he drew them down my legs and over my feet. Then he prised my legs apart. Flipping his loose nightshirt upwards, he placed himself above me and got between my legs. I continued to struggle and thrash about, but he was too powerful for me. The next thing I knew, I was experiencing a searing pain as his manhood tried to force itself in between my legs. I felt a hot liquid trickle down and intense pain as he thrust himself deep inside me and began a steady up and down movement. He held my breast meanwhile, and grunted, saying how beautiful I was. I was now past the point of struggle. I was tired and weak and I lay there, not quite sure what was happening to me, until I heard him scream 'Oh my God!', and then he rolled off me on to the bed, exhausted. I jumped out of the bed. There was a toilet adjoining the bedroom and I went in there to wash. When I returned, I noticed that there was blood on the bedsheet next to where Mr Mana lay. He watched me as I came from the bathroom and said, 'I hope I can trust you. Don't tell anyone what has happened. Be a good girl.' I heard him; but my hand was already on the doorknob. I turned the key, opened the door and ran into my room and lay down. I was very depressed. A myriad of thoughts ran through my mind. What would Mrs Mana say if she knew what had happened? Why had Mr Mana, whom I regarded as a god, done that to me? What would the children, Sarah and Paulina, say if they knew what their daddy had done to me? I was confused, perplexed.

All that morning, I lay in my bed and cried my heart out. I cried myself to sleep. 'Lemma!' I heard, and opened my eyes. It was Mr Mana. 'It's time to go for the children.' I ignored the call, closed my eyes. After a while, I heard him say, 'I'm going for the children. Lock the front door please. Make my bed.' I lay still in bed.

After he had gone, I went to lock the front door. It was only then I remembered that I had left my panties in Mr Mana's bedroom. I went there and tried the lock. It was open. I went in and found that he had not changed the bedsheet. My panties were lying on the bed. I grabbed them and took the stained bedsheet away and quickly put on another sheet, then went out of the room, greatly relieved. I went to the general bathroom which I shared with the children, washed the panties, the bedsheet, the dress I had been wearing, and had my bath. I placed all the things out on the clothes-line to dry. Then I went back to my bed. I picked up a book but could not read. My depression had still not left me. I wished I could sleep but was not able to do so. I lay there with my thoughts. I wished my mother had been around. Maybe, I would have been able to ask her some questions. But she was far away. I knew that I could never discuss what had happened with Mrs Mana. I could not make a disclosure. I had no friend older than myself with whom I could discuss it. I felt extremely lonely.

After what seemed like hours, the doorbell rang and I went to answer it. Sarah and Paulina had returned. The latter rushed in, as was usual with her. 'Guess what happened at school today!' she said excitedly as she dashed into her room to deposit her school bag. I followed her, happy to find something that took my thoughts away from my immediate worries.

'Don't listen to her,' urged Sarah with a smile. 'It's a school secret.'

'It's no secret,' replied Paulina. 'Just guess what happened.'

When I did not reply, they both laughed.

'It was the school farm,' Paulina exalted.

I did not know there was a school farm.

'Well, it's not a farm,' Sarah said. 'It's a poultry.'

'And my chicken laid an egg!' Paulina cried.

'That wasn't your chicken. It was mine.'

'No, it was mine.' Paulina insisted. 'Mine is brown, remember, and yours black and white.'

'What was so special about the egg? After all, several chickens have been laying eggs.'

'But mine had not laid one. That's what's special. And when I touched the egg, it was warm, very warm.'

Ha! ha! ha! ha! The children laughed, filling with sunshine and cheer.

'It's lunch-time,' I said. 'What would you like to have?'

'Plantain and stew,' said Paulina.

'Rice and stew with banana,' Sarah chose.

'All right, in ten minutes,' I said, and hurried off to the kitchen. I was pleased that Mr Mana was nowhere in sight. He had apparently come in, gone upstairs and then left the house.

Sarah and Paulina had their lunch and after that decided that they wanted a walk before they went for the piano lessons which a lady on the estate offered them once a week.

I stayed with them all afternoon as a way of working off my

depression. But it would not go away. When Mrs Mana returned that evening, she noticed that something was amiss with me.

'What's the matter, Lemma?' she asked.

I wished I could tell her the truth. But I was not able.

'I'm a bit troubled,' I said.

'Fever? Malaria?'

'No. I think it's my period.'

'Ah. I can understand your depression. Take some paracetamol. It's in the cupboard in the bathroom. You'll feel better.'

'Thank you, Mrs Mana.'

'A woman's personal problem. God, in his wisdom, gave us the pain which no man will ever experience. And this pain, no woman can ever fail to experience. It's good for you, Lemma,' she joked.

Good for me or not, I found myself at the mercy of Mr Mana. From that first day when he raped me on, he had me whenever he wanted me. And each time he spent a week in the house, he ensured that he took me once or twice. It was always a furtive affair, because he was scared stiff of his wife and did not want the children or anyone else to know. He always swore to me how much he loved me, how ravishing I was, how beautiful, how he would like to have me for ever. And then he began to ply me with gifts. Looking back now, I find that he gave me nothing really. But in those days, an earring, a handkerchief, sweets, chocolates, all such things pleased me a great deal. I was not experienced in the ways of the world, otherwise I'd have known that he was exploiting me. He had sexual satisfaction, and he did not have to work hard for it; I was at his beck and call and I came cheap, even by market value, very cheap. I thought about it in later years, and I felt particularly bad. I had been exploited. And it's not that he was an exciting sexual partner, either. I just did not know anything about sex. No one had spoken to me about it, and no one had taught me anything of it. I was to realize much, much later what a terrible sexual partner he was.

But at that time, he thrilled me. I found myself waiting for his call, and if it did not come soon after his arrival for his week-long stay, I felt offended. There was even a thrill in knowing that I was sharing the same bed as Mrs Mana, so that when she got on her high horse with me, I often felt superior to her. If only she had known what was what she could not have bullied me at all.

This went on for all of six months and more. But it could not remain under wraps for ever. For my part, I was beginning to beautify myself, wearing Mrs Mana's perfumes surreptitiously, and sporting new earrings and bangles, for which Mrs Mana could not account. She tried to find out if I had acquired a boyfriend, but I denied it, and she had no evidence that I was going out with anybody. In addition, there developed a certain familiarity between me and Mr Mana. I think it inescapable. Once a man and a woman become intimate, all barriers break down; gently at first and then completely, depending on the strength of their passion. The age difference does not matter, nor does class or disparity in their situations. The woman has a certain hold over the man, in which he is captive. And the woman, being woman, will exert her right to conquest in so many ways. I believe Mrs Mana knew that and when she began to suspect me with her husband, she laid the trap. Presto, we fell into it. She caught us red-handed and all hell was let loose.

Not on me and Mr Mana together. Not on Mr Mana, by any means. On me. Lemona. Slut. Prostitute. Husband-snatcher. She had brought me from the mud of the creeks, put clothes on me, shoes on my feet, food in my stomach, taught me how to do dishes, cook and sweep, enabled me to ride in a car, put me in the company of a decent family and other decent people. And what did I turn round and do? Abuse the goodness of her heart. Introduce my prostitute ways into her family. I was about to ruin her lovely, young girls. No doubt, I had begun to introduce them to the trade. Was she not foolish to have allowed me to share the same room with the tender fruits of her own womb? She had provided me with a bed and a mattress and sheets and pillows on which to sleep, so far away from the mat and hard mound for which I was best suited and created. Was I content with that? No. I had to go and desecrate her marital bed. Her marital bed! And she, Mrs Mana, would have to put up with the shame of that for the rest of her life. If I were some educated woman, of the same class as herself, she might have lived it down. But a house-girl, possessed of no education whatsoever, a bastard if ever there was one, having nothing besides beautiful figure and face, had dared to cheat on her, dared to ruin a marriage which she had done so much to maintain against all the odds. Well, she was not going to blame me; it was all her fault. She had given me an inch in the first place, treated me like a human being, whereas I was a bitch, as hot as they come. There was only one thing for it – return me to the mud from which she had extricated me. I could go there and splash about in the filth of my mind, and she'd see how I would extricate myself therefrom. I was proof of the old adage, a woman could never be better than her mother. My mother was unmarried and had me by a man who did not greet her after mating with her. I was following in her footsteps. I was about to ruin the reputation of her dear husband. How would he face their family friends when they knew that he was sleeping with his nanny? Oh the temptations women bring to men! Well, there was just one thing for it. I had to leave the house. Clear it of my corruption and stench. And do it quickly before her lovely children inhaled the pollution I had spread about. She would have to use the most corrosive disinfectant money could buy to rid her house and family of my putrefaction. And I would pack my lousy things into the case she had given me – I was lucky she was a woman of good upbringing otherwise she would have made me return to my wretched mother with the same little bundle of tattered second-hand clothes I'd brought. And I would have to leave immediately. She would make darned sure that I got into a bus that would take me directly to my wretched village lest I should duck and return to my tryst with her husband. There were a lot of men on earth, God knew, and why did not single girls go after single men? Why would they insist on sharing another woman's man? Tears. Hysteria. Was I packed and ready? Hurry up, slut, prostitute, bitch, thief.

Deep down inside me, I hurt, and hurt badly too. But you would not have guessed it from my face. I did not utter a word throughout her tirade. I absorbed every word, every thrust of her dagger, deflected every missile she directed at me until she exhausted herself. I could not blame her. Nor did I particularly blame myself. The culprit was quiet through all this. He locked himself into his room, and you would not have thought he had a hand in the storm. I have since thought how lucky men are to be able to have women offer them pleasure and contentment on a platter of gold – most of the time.

I was already packing the few things I had. It did not take me any time at all. I had a bit of money, enough to enable me travel to Dukana, I thought, and to spend for some time. Some of that money had been given to me by Mr Mana. The rest were gifts I had had from Mrs Mana's friends, for whom I ran errands on occasion. It all came to nothing, really. I had not thought of putting money aside for anything – I was well provided for in the Mana household.

I walked into the lounge, where Mrs Mana was already waiting for me. I did not look at her. I knew she would be livid. I walked out of the lounge behind her. Outside the door, she opened the car door for me. I got in. She banged the door and drove me to the bus station. I alighted there. She gave me a few pounds, as my transport fare back to Dukana, which I accepted. And she was gone.

I bought a few things for mother and boarded a lorry for Dukana. The journey was uneventful. I kept myself to myself, barely answering the greetings that a few people who knew me threw. I had grown a lot in the three years since I left Dukana and some of the passengers from there hardly recognized me.

I arrived home at dusk to the boredom which I had left behind three years earlier. Dukana was no different from the village I had known, indeed, it was decidedly worse. Familiarity with the life of the township made the village seem like a death sentence. And I knew I would not stay there for long.

CHAPTER FOUR

Mama Bomboy

Mother was on her deathbed when I arrived. In the three years of my absence, illness, hunger and hopelessness had taken their toll on her. She had always been a frail woman, but now she was emaciated beyond recognition. Nor was she able to recognize me. Her carcase lay by a fire, wracked by a cough that sounded like a talking drum. The sight of her drove me to despair.

For one week, I fulfilled the obligations of a daughter, tending her, speaking to her, hoping that she would recognize me and say a word or two to me. But all my efforts were futile. Mother was far gone.

A fortnight after my arrival, she gave up the ghost at night. I woke up to find that she was no longer breathing. Heartbreaking as it was, I considered that fate had done her a favour. It had been no life at all; better it was terminated than that it should drag out to no purpose.

We buried her in the house where she had lived that very morning. There was no ceremony. I was the only one weeping tears as we laid her on a mat in her final resting place. The men covered the grave, I bought them a few drinks, and it was all over. There would be none of the other ceremonies normally associated with death in Dukana. I could not afford it, and mother left nothing.

I remained in Dukana for another week, during which a number of people called on me to offer their condolences. Again, many could not recognize in me the little girl whom they had known three years earlier. Even my own friends remarked on how much I had bloomed in those years. I was already a woman. If I stayed longer in Dukana someone was bound to ask for my hand in marriage. The mere thought convinced me that I should not stay a day longer in the village. What would I be doing being a Dukana wife? I would end up just like my mother. No, I was not meant to live in the village. My life was in the township. And it was to that life I bent my mind and my footsteps.

I combed the house thoroughly for any items of value that might be given out. There was nothing. I burnt mother's few clothes and, on an impulse, took the only durable thing I found – the knife she normally used to cut the yam seedlings before planting. It was a little knife, a shade bigger than a penknife but with a sharp point and edges. It had a wooden handle. That was the only memento of my mother I found. I remembered her using it, and I thought that keeping it would always remind me of her. I threw it into the bottom of my suitcase.

Three weeks to the day after my arrival in Dukana, I was once again headed for Port Harcourt, now with the case I had been given, but otherwise much poorer than when I had left the township.

It was only when I got into the lorry that I thought about where I would be going to in Port Harcourt. And I could not find an answer. Indeed, I had not one friend there. Now, I said to myself, did I have a friend in Dukana? I took a final look at the house in which I had been born and where I had been reared. I knew that the next rains could crumble it and there would no longer be a reminder of the family. Poverty would have dealt my family a final blow, more so if I, the last of the line, was unable to pull through life and make something of myself. As the rickety lorry pulled away, I cast a last, remorseless look on the village. I was happy that I had no further links with the wretched place.

But what did the future hold for me? To that question, there was no easy answer. I had no education to speak of, although I could read and write a little; I had no skills beyond the ordinary housekeeping ability which I had acquired with the Manas; and no money. But I was, as I had been told, strikingly beautiful and hard-working. Could beauty and a capacity for hard work earn me a decent living? Give me success in life? I was little past sixteen years. Had no experience. And now I think of it, that was a clear disadvantage. What could a sixteen-year-old without a father, mother, relations, friends, education, skill, do in a township like Port Harcourt, which was full of strangers and where jobs were not easy to come by? I had also made up my mind that I would not be a nanny to anyone. After Mrs Mana, I would have been insane to go to live with another family. Certainly, there would be a husband who, unable to resist my looks, would take advantage of me. And I would not be able to help myself because I would want to protect my job and the husband's honour. No, I was finished with being a house-help. And, by the way, Mr Mana had not paid me in the three years I lived with him. Nor had he sent money to my late mother. Or had he? Could he have been sending what was due to me end-month to her? There was now no way of knowing. Mother was dead and buried. Nor did I care to know, for that matter. I was finished with the Manas. Much good may they come to. I'd miss the young girls, Sarah and Paulina; they were ever so smart and chatty! But that had to be forgotten, buried, like mother. Never recall it. The future was what mattered. And that future would start the moment the lorry stopped at the Port Harcourt motor park.

In two hours, that wobbly future started. I still had not sorted out what to do on arrival. I was stranded. The moment I got out of the lorry, like a crab deserted by the tide on a sandy seashore. I stood there, suitcase in hand, unsure what to do or where to go. Taxis, bicycles, pedestrians, whirled past me. I looked about for a face I might recognize. I hoped that someone might recognize me. No one did. One hour had passed. Then, on an impulse, I remembered the hairdressers in the market. One of them, Mama Bomboy as she was nicknamed, used to fuss over me each time I went to have my hair plaited. She would surely be pleased to see me. And since her shed was a popular meeting place for the women of Port Harcourt of some class, I might find assistance from one of her customers.

I dragged myself there slowly. The moment she set eyes on me, Mama Bomboy became ecstatic. 'My daughter, welcome. I didn't see you last month. You didn't come to have your hair done. What happened? You are looking as beautiful as ever. My God, you are a be-au-ti-ful girl. A beauty queen! You should take part in a beauty competition. You would win! Welcome.'

The statement, rendered in pidgin English, was very colourful, arresting, and brought a smile to my face, and to the customers waiting their turn in her shed and other hairdressers' sheds. Mama Bomboy always spoke in a loud voice.

She was a large woman, with generous breasts, powerful arms and an enormous posterior, which wiggled and waggled as she walked. She would not have been more than forty or forty-two years old, but she had lived a rough life, and it showed on her face and her hands. The ample supply of hair on her head was carefully and elegantly braided. She was busy when I arrived, and after pouring her admiration of me into the market place, continued her work on her customer's head. I found a seat on the bench in the shed. Hunger gnawed at my entrails, and I went off briefly to buy myself some groundnuts and bananas and a soft drink.

On my return, Mama Bomboy had finished with her customer and was seated in her shed. As soon as I entered she asked if I had come to have my hair plaited.

'No,' I answered, pointing to the suitcase.

'Are you travelling?'

'No,' I replied. 'I've just returned from the village.'

'The village? You are no longer living here with Mrs Mana?'

'No. I left her about a month ago.'

'One month! And she didn't mention it when she came here a fortnight ago to have her hair plaited. What happened?'

'It's along story, Mama Bomboy. I can't tell it here.'

'Eia! Eia! My poor daughter. Why have you come back here then?'

'I returned to my mother in the village. But she died a week ago.'

'Eia! Eia! My poor daughter. And what about your father?'

'I never had a father,' I replied.

'Never had a father? What d'you mean? Everyone must have a father. Even Jesus had a father.'

'I meant to say my father did not marry my mother. They were not man and wife, and my mother never introduced him to me.'

'Eia! Eia! My poor daughter.'

'D'you have any relatives?'

'No.'

35

'Not in the village?'

'No.'

'Not in town here?'

'No.'

'So, where are you going to stay? Why did you leave the village for this wretched place called a township?'

'There was nowhere else to go.'

'So, where are you going to stay now that you've returned?'

'I don't know, Mama. That's why I came to see you.'

'Don't you have any friends here?'

'No, Mama.'

'Eia! Eia! My poor daughter. What will happen to you?'

You could see that she was agitated, genuinely distressed. And from the way she worked her face, I imagined that she was thinking what to do in the circumstances. After a while, she said. 'Wait here with me until the day is over. I'll see what I can do.'

Not one to sit idly by while there was work to do, I began to assist in plaiting the hair of the next customers who called. That was one thing I could do, and do very well. Like all Dukana girls, I had been at it since I was a child. I plaited the hair of the Mana daughters, Sarah and Paulina, for all the three years I was with them. What money I saved the family thereby! And it gave me pleasure twisting the thread round the hair and making various patterns and styles to fit different heads and faces. There was art in it, and it pleased me to exert myself in this way. I worked hard all that afternoon, and I could see that Mama Bomboy was very pleased with me.

At dusk, the market began to empty, and the hairdressers without customers started to pack up, ready to leave for their homes. I tidied up Mama Bomboy's shed, sweeping the hair and threads away, and soon, we were on our way to her residence.

She lived on Niger Street, within easy walking distance of the market, in what was known as Old Port Harcourt, that part which had been well laid-out by the white men who founded the town. I had heard Mrs Mana, who grew up in the area, speak of it, and we had often gone there with the children to see her mother. The houses were built dormitory-style, as single rooms, with doors linking them. Behind the rooms was an open-space courtyard facing the cooking area, common bathroom and common toilet. Tenants hired single rooms or as many single rooms as they desired, and were free to use or lock the connecting doors as they pleased. The families being large, there was an enormous number of people in each house.

As we walked home with the things Mama Bomboy had bought for the household that day, she told me that I was free to stay with her for as long as I pleased. She felt sure that her husband would not object to my staying with them. He was quite old, she said, and felt sure that he would not place me under the sort of pressure which, she was sure, had made me leave the Manas.

'Don't ask me how I knew, my daughter, I am a woman and can see that your beautiful face and extraordinary figure, coupled with your youth and inexperience, are meat for wolves to eat. I will tell you more about that later.'

'Yes, Mama.'

We walked on in silence. Yes, Mama. I turned the phrase over in my mind. It sounded somewhat strange, and yet so familiar, usual. Was I in need of a mother all over again? But a mother different from the natural one I had just buried? Or was it a real mother who knew the ways of the world and who could advise a teenaged daughter on how to get along? Mama Bomboy. So called because her first child, a son, was nicknamed 'Bomboy', some meaningless name. He was already grown-up and was away at university. The next boy was in boarding school; only the two girls were home. Both were younger than me. Mama Bomboy told me all that, by way of introduction to the family, as we walked to her house.

The street was busy, that time of day. People were returning from their day's chores either at the wharf, the market, the offices, or from their travels. Buses, taxis, motor cycles and bicycles passed us at varying speed. Hawkers of food – plantain, maize, fish and meat – had their tripods and fires out and were busy cooking, in preparation for their nightly customers.

When we got to Mama Bomboy's, I was introduced to the two girls, Ifeoma and Nkiru, both of them attending day secondary schools in Port Harcourt. Mama Bomboy made me feel at home immediately. 'We don't have much, and we do not live like the Manas as you can see, but you are welcome to all we have. Papa Bomboy will be returning soon. I'm sure he'll welcome you too.'

We shared the housework and were done in no time at all. I had dinner with the girls, Mama Bomboy choosing to await the arrival of her husband.

The family lived in two rooms, with a connecting door. One room was used as bedroom by man and wife, the other room was parlour in the daytime and bedroom for the girls at night. They laid a foam mattress on the cement floor, overlaid it with mat and pillow, and slept there. I had to share the floor with them. I was quite content. We had to retire early so that the girls could wake up in time for school, and I was tired after the day's exertions.

But before that, Papa Bomboy, a man in his late fifties, arrived and was duly introduced to the new addition to the household. He only said, 'Welcome. God bless you.'

The daily routine at Mama Bomboy's was fairly predictable. We all woke up early, the girls to prepare for school, and I for the market. General cleaning of the rooms was followed by our going some distance to fetch water at the pump, then we had a bath, and the girls had breakfast and were off to school at about six thirty. We, Mama Bomboy and I, left for the market a few minutes later, without breakfast.

There was not much to do in the morning hours. Customers didn't begin to arrive until towards noon. But we would sit there, all the same, conversing. All the hairdressers were in one row of sheds, and all of them, women, had a lot of gossip to share. Almost always, it was about their experiences as women, the family, the children, their men, men, relationships between men and women. It was a new world entirely for me, and there was a lot for me to learn. No experiences were ever the same, but the tenor of their conversation was the heavy burden they had to bear as women.

Once the customers began to trickle in, we were invariably very busy. While I was at the Manas', I had on every occasion to wait for my turn because Mama Bomboy worked alone. With my arrival, business was more brisk. I tended to encourage a larger clientele, possibly because they found I was quite deft at plaiting, braiding or weaving their hair.

In between customers, I would find time to have a meal – invariably bean cake, with the water we brought from home, or groundnuts and bananas. Mama Bomboy would normally give me some money for this light meal.

We would return home at the end of the day for the only real meal we had, and exhausted, I would go to bed.

It was an exciting new experience. I was doing something I enjoyed, and Mama Bomboy was very supportive. She praised me to the skies. We worked all week, including Sundays. And at the end of the month, Mama Bomboy paid me. I forget how much now, but it was not much. However, I valued what I was paid as much as the goodness behind it. And when I thought that the Manas had not paid me anything after three years of slaving for them, I regarded Mama Bomboy as an angel.

I had been with her for three months when one day, following a lull in activity in the shed, Mama Bomboy came and sat next to me and called, 'Lemma.'

'Yes, Mama.'

'You have been here three months now. Do you like it?'

'I do, Mama Bomboy.'

'I'm happy for you, and glad that I was able to help you when you needed that help most.'

My heart missed a beat. I hoped that she was not about to stop me from working with her, staying with her. Although I worked seven days a week and did not have the opportunity for socializing, I was learning a lot in the market, meeting other women, listening to new ideas, and by association with Mama's daughters, making new friends. I still relied very much on the goodwill of Mama Bomboy. I could not do without it.

'Thank you, Mama Bomboy,' I asserted. 'I'm very grateful to you.'

'Eia, my poor daughter. You have been most helpful and I, too, am grateful to you. But I am mother enough to ask myself how long you can stay here helping me to plait women's hair. And I'm woman enough to know that with your face and figure, you will soon be open to many choices. You are a very beautiful girl, Lemona. I have watched you awake and asleep, my daughter, and I have to confess that I have not yet seen such a well-sculpted face on a girl, a woman. You have liquid, dancing eyes, small, long eyelashes, a small, pointed nose, small lips covering a set of pearl-white teeth, a smooth, rounded face, perfect, silk-soft skin, a long neck and long, slim fingers.'

I blushed and looked down at my feet. Mama Bomboy continued her praise sing, although I wished she would stop, so embarrassed was I.

'You have a perfect figure, pointed, bra-bursting, erect breasts, a slim waist, wide hips, a perfectly formed pelvis, long legs and small feet. You are, in short, an elegant woman. God could not have created you better, had he made you in his very image. Your movement is that of a gazelle, an antelope, graceful and tantalizing. If I find one fault in you, it's probably in a slight bow in your legs, but that is nothing. Only those who observe you very closely will ever notice it. And it is this extraordinary beauty of form which worries me about you. You don't have a proper school education, although I can see you are hard-working, and could very easily have finished school if you had had the opportunity. Lacking that, I have wondered what the future holds for you.'

Here she paused and drew a deep breath.

'Lemona, you are woman. You are growing up, and will soon be face to face with all the problems women face. For what is a woman, I ask. Beautiful, she is at the beck and call of every man who will try to take advantage of her. Ugly, she is most likely at the mercy of a man who will none the less find in her something of value – her character, upbringing or something intangible which only he knows. In either case, the lot of a woman is to slave for the man. To provide his pleasure, bear and rear his children. If she is brilliant, she will subordinate her career to the rearing of a family, fetching and carrying for her husband and children, and may not do as well as she ought to have done for herself. Lucky is the gifted woman who finds a husband who supports her. Otherwise, her lot is to find herself envied and subdued, subjugated by a man who feels she cannot, should not, be better than himself.

Successful, she has to carry her torch for, if she is working, her career, her husband, her children, her family, her home, so she does five jobs at one and the same time. Otherwise, if she finds a successful career, she cannot fulfil her obligations to her family and she loses her man. A woman is thought not to be complete until she has a man for whom she hungers by nature and a child or children to bring her fulfilment. But what does she get from them? Love at first when she is young and desirable to her man, but when she gets older, her husband begins to go dancing around town, looking for younger women. And her children, as soon as they grow up and establish their independence, either forget her or are so inundated by their personal problems that they have no time for their ageing mother who must perforce keep thinking of them and wishing them well. A woman may become a mother to a son; the moment he marries, his wife is his mother's antagonist, a competitor for her love. If she's mother to a daughter, the moment she marries, her husband dislikes her mother, and may not welcome her to their marital home. If a woman does not marry, she is immediately the object of vile gossip, is thought of as irresponsible, may not go to a party or a dance on her own, is regarded as available to any spindly-legged man walking on two feet in a pair of trousers. Alone she'll be if she has no children, growing old without support. Should she choose to be a single parent, she's racked by all the problems of rearing children single-handedly: boys who demand the authority of a father, or girls who need a father-figure. A woman in love is lost to one man, whose heart may flutter at the sight of a skirt, and soon she finds she's sharing her man, and disappointment comes drooping to her with stooping shoulders. And she may soon find herself part of a harem, hoping and praying that her man will find her some time in the week. She has to cook and slave for him, and deck herself out in an attempt, sometimes vain, to secure and maintain even his divided attention. Come old age, and a woman is but a rag on a peg. A man at ninety may find a much younger woman to marry, take pleasure in love and sex, may still be able to father children – but which woman at sixty still found sexual pleasure, could bear children and had a man at her feet? She may yet spend the last twenty or thirty years of her life without the loving feel of a warm heart beating against hers, or a loving arm around her shoulders. So, in desperation or out of pure necessity, a woman turns to her kind for support. Does she get it? No. It's all gossip and more gossip, envy or jealousy. Racked and tortured by the demands of society, or her own contrary nature, a woman is a plaything in the hands of fate. That is why, my poor daughter, I fear for you. Your great beauty, this wonderful endowment of nature, may prove your undoing. But it may yet be a blessing, for you are better with it than without. It may ease your passage through life. For you will not lack the company of men. May the right man or men turn up and may you yourself choose right when that time comes.'

She stopped and stood up and embraced me long. There were tears in her eyes. I cannot say that I understood all she said at the time but I have since ruminated over that speech and found the wisdom in most of what she said. Some of my experience has borne her out. But are we ever guided by the wise words we hear? Isn't wisdom to be appreciated only with the twenty-twenty vision of hindsight? And are we in control of all aspects of our life? Who knows what fate, nature, decrees for each of us? If we knew, would we believe it? That day, all I found in my life was the one question, 'Mama Bomboy, do you love your husband, and does Papa Bomboy love you?'

She looked at me fondly and sighed. 'We have a life together, that's all I can say. We have children and we are bringing them up together, to the best of our ability.'

I did not find those words particularly comforting. I had stayed with the family for three months and found some happiness, and thought that all was light and sweetness, since I had not heard a quarrel or a harsh word. Now, here I was before Mama Bomboy, and she was painting a harsh picture of a woman's life. Had she had a difficult life? Were her words the result of her life experience? I did not know at the time, and have not been able to find out.

After that day, things moved rapidly for me, and not by my making either. I spent another three months with Mama Bomboy, and after a while, began to find the work boring and without a future, as Mama Bomboy had accurately predicted. I did not see myself plaiting hair all my life. Most of the hairdressers in the market, I noticed, were married women trying to increase the family income. If so, the marital state was important. In both houses where I had stayed, a man and a woman were together bringing up children. It looked important. Besides, the example of my mother, who had found neither help nor support in sickness, was there to warn me at all times. I began to find myself yearning for something different, for company, possibly male company.

I have already said that several women, in all stations of life, came to the shed to have their hair done. It was through this that I met Maybel, or Ineh, who was to lead me on to the next stage in my life.

CHAPTER FIVE

Maybel

She came on a Sunday afternoon to the shed. Stocky and sturdily built, I would say that she was plain. She did not have much hair on her head, and I was alone that day, Mama Bomboy having chosen not to work. I had barely started work on Maybel's head when she asked me what my name was.

'Lemona,' I replied.

'I'm called Ineh, but most of my friends call me Maybel. You are a very pretty girl, or is it woman?'

'Thank you very much.' I twisted thread round her hair.

'What are you doing here?'

'Braiding your hair, madam.'

'Don't call me "madam", please. I'm Maybel – M-a-y-b-e-l, not M-a-b-e-l. Understand?'

'Yes, Maybel.'

'Sweet. Real sweet. Give me a mirror, let me see what's happening to the hair on the back of my head. No, hold it. How long have you been doing this?'

'A few months.'

'Are you well paid doing it?'

'You don't pay much for a plait, do you? So I cannot be well paid. But I'm all right.'

'When a few months stretch to one year, two years, are you still going to be plaiting people's hair?' Maybel asked.

'That's the question everyone has asked me. It's as though they all want me to stop doing it.'

'Do you like doing it?'

'I do. I enjoy it. But then it cannot be what I'll do for ever,' I replied. 'It was all right when I came and needed all the help in the world. Now ... well ...'

'Tell me all about it,' Maybel urged.

'It's a long story and this is no place for it.'

'Darling, you must come and tell me the story, no matter how long it is. My name is Maybel Suku. You must have heard of me.'

'No, I haven't.'

'Sugar! You must be new in town. By the way, how old are you?'

'About seventeen,' I giggled.

'Sugar! I didn't know you were so young. You look twenty-one. A big seventeen you are! No wonder you haven't heard of Maybel Suku. Here's my card. I'm a businesswoman. Come and see me next Sunday. You don't work every Sunday, do you?'

'Yes.'

'Sugar! Take next Sunday off anyway. Tell your Mama. I'm sure she'll let you go. One Sunday in a month won't ruin her business. And come and see me. My address is on the card. My flat is on the second floor. Come about ten o'clock in the morning. We'll spend the day together. Right, darling?'

'Thank you.'

She paid for the hair-do and gave me a heavy tip, saying, 'Your fare to my place next Sunday. Be sure to come. Ask for Maybel Suku, darling. Bye now.'

She walked off confidently, with a swagger in her step. I saw her get into a car and drive off. Confidence. I was impressed, very impressed. I looked forward to meeting her on the Sunday, as she had proposed.

All week, I thought of nothing but Maybel. Her confidence, her self-assurance, her interest in me. Who was she anyway? Businesswoman, she had said she was. What exactly did that mean? I told Mama Bomboy as early as Tuesday that I would like the Sunday off.

'Why?' she asked, surprised.

'I wish to visit someone.'

'Who is that?'

'Her name is Maybel Suku.'

'How do you know her?'

'She came to have her hair done last Sunday and when I was through, she invited me to come over to her place next Sunday.'

'What does she do?' Mama asked.

'Said she's a businesswoman. Drives a car. I think she lives in an upstairs building.'

'I see,' Mama Bomboy said. 'Yes, you can have the Sunday off. But be careful. This is a township. People are not what they seem.'

I asked around in my very limited circles, but no one could tell me who Maybel Suku was. So I had to wait until the Sunday to satisfy my curiosity. Nor did Sunday arrive early enough. The days kept dragging, interminably so! Finally, Saturday turned up and trailed its lame feet all twenty-four hours of the day. I did my work quite shoddily.

I was up early on Sunday and got dressed even before everyone was fully awake. It was as though I were going to meet a new lover. I even applied a bit of make-up to my eyes and lips – a thing I had not done since I arrived at Mama Bomboy's. The prospect of the visit excited me a great deal and I was keen to arrive there on time lest I should miss Maybel. The way she behaved at our first meeting, I thought that if I went later than the time she stipulated, I might not find her in.

She had given me enough money to take a taxi ride to her place, which was in the New Layout area of the town. I arrived a quarter of an hour before ten o'clock. I climbed the stairs and rang the doorbell. She answered it herself, opening the door and wrapping me in a warm embrace. She was still in her nightgown and dressing gown. 'Welcome, darling Lemona,' she said in honeyed tones, and motioned me to a seat.

The lounge was well-appointed, and the colours of the curtains, settee and carpet matched. On the wall were several pictures, all enlarged, and also two paintings, framed.

'Come on, let's go to the kitchen. I was about to prepare breakfast. Have you had breakfast?'

'No,' I replied.'

'Well, then, we'll breakfast together.'

She swept me into the kitchen, and I helped her break the eggs and then set the table. In a short while, we were at the breakfast table. I had a proper breakfast for the first time since I left the Mana household.

After that, she excused herself, saying she needed to have a bath and get dressed. I waited in the lounge, listening to music on the large radiogram which she had in the lounge. It was obvious that Maybel was a woman of some means. There was no sign of a man around the house.

Maybel soon swept into the lounge once again, all dressed and made up. We got talking, or she got me to talk. But I had made up my mind that I was not going tell her about my experience at the Manas'. I only told her of my upbringing in Dukana, the incomplete primary-school education I had had, my determination to live in a township and my disgust with the insipid life of the village. My life with Mama Bomboy, I asserted, was in lieu of a better one and I would be quite happy if I found something else to do. The main problem, I said, was that I had not been trained to do anything else.

'We'll see what we can do about that,' she said, agreeably to my ears.

Then she told me how she had trained abroad as a teacher and had taught in a government secondary school upon her return to the country. After a while, she had got bored with teaching and had decided to branch out on her own, following in the footsteps of her parents, both of whom were business people. She had established her business five years earlier, and considered herself something of a success, although she still expected to do much better. She had received quite some support from her parents, which probably, she asserted, explained part of her success, although the other part was another story altogether.

She invited me on a tour of the flat. First, her bedroom, well laid out, with clean sheets and flower-patterned pillow slips. Her wardrobe was full to bursting, definitely richer than Mrs Mana's, and she had a great array of shoes in different colours, all carefully set out and pointing in one direction. The dressing table would have pleased any cosmetologist: a great number of creams, lipsticks in various shades, perfumes of varied fragrances. I asked and was allowed to spray some of the perfume on myself. The bathroom was very neatly kept and smelt fresh and fragrant. The kitchen I had already seen to be extremely neat and orderly, with pots and pans gleaming as though they had just been purchased. Finally, we went to the guest bedroom, which was separated from Maybel's own bedroom by the common bathroom. This was also well furnished but had obviously not been lived in for a long time. It appeared to be waiting for an occupant.

We had completed a tour of the flat when the doorbell rang, and Maybel went to answer it. She opened the door and welcomed another female – a little older than me, I guessed. Maybel introduced her to me as Uche, a friend of hers.

We sat together and chatted, or should I say, I listened to Maybel and Uche discuss something pertaining to land and the Ministry of Works at Enugu, the regional headquarters. Apparently, Maybel had sent Uche on an errand to that city. They discussed at some length, and then Maybel decided that we should all go for a ride in her car.

We trooped downstairs and got into the Volkswagen Beetle. Maybel told me she had bought it from a European who was leaving the country. Uche sat next to her on the front seat while I found a place at the back. We drove out of town to the Imo river bridge, where Maybel haggled over and bought some fresh fish, then to her parents' place in Diobu, a run-down, thickly populated part of Port Harcourt. She gave the fish she had bought to her mother, who prepared us a late lunch. Then she drove me to Mama Bomboy's, leaving me at the front of the house after giving me a peck on both cheeks. 'You should come over to the house next Saturday. I believe Sunday is a busy day for you in the market, so your Mama may not allow you out again on another Sunday. Will you come?'

'Yes,' I said, without hesitation.

'Promise?'

'I promise.'

'Good night, Lemona.' From Maybel and Uche, almost in unison.

'Good night, Maybel, good night, Uche.'

I was flushed with excitement. I went over the day's activity as I lay in bed, having skipped dinner with the family since I was quite full. Maybel was a very exciting person and I was pleased that she had extended me an invitation for later in the week. She was going to be a very valuable friend, I thought.

The next day, while at the market, Mama Bomboy made me recount all that had happened at Maybel's. She must have noticed the excited way in which I retold my experiences.

'Did she say what sort of business she's in?'

'No, I didn't ask her.'

'You must remember to ask when you next meet her.'

'She's invited me next Saturday. You will allow me to go, won't you, please, Mama Bomboy?'

'Certainly, my daughter.'

'Oh, thank you. Thank you very much. I do like Maybel so.'

'You don't know her enough yet. Don't get over-excited. This is a township. It has all sorts of characters.'

Maybel, I found, was indeed a character. I spent the next Saturday with her and many other Saturdays after that. There was not a dull moment in her company, no matter how long we spent together. She introduced me to Port Harcourt, its sights and sounds, and I was truly grateful to her for giving me insights I might never have had but for her.

Inevitably, our relationship grew, and she invited me to live with her. The offer pleased me a great deal and I thanked her for it. But it was going to be difficult for me to part with Mama Bomboy and her family. She had been of immense help to me and I had found kindness, understanding and support at her hands.

However, when I proposed to leave, she did not hesitate to let me go. She gave me her blessing and hoped that I would make a success of my life. From what I had told her, she believed that Maybel, my new friend, would offer me far more opportunities than she could ever have done, and wished me luck in my new situation.

'Are you going to work for her?' she asked.

'I don't know. She doesn't have an office as far as I can see, but I'll be able to learn from what she does and maybe get busy on my own. I think I could do some business after I have understudied her.'

'Be careful, Lemona. Be careful. If you ever have any problems, anyway, you know I'm here to help. I have no money, and cannot help you with money, but experience and advice I do have and those I can give you for free.'

I had been with Mama Bomboy for almost a year. When I left, it was a very emotional occasion. Mama's two daughters helped me put my things in my suitcase and saw me off into the taxi which took me to Maybel's. There were a lot of tears at the parting.

Years after, I was to look back on that year with nostalgia. It was probably the only time I met with humane treatment. When no one tried to exploit me, take advantage of me or misuse me. Alas, Mama Bomboy was not to be there when later I had difficulties, and she was the only person to whom I could have turned in my hour of need for honest, useful advice. She died peacefully in her sleep a few months after I left her house. I attended her simple funeral with Maybel.

I moved into Maybel's spare bedroom on a friendship basis. My understanding was that she would gradually introduce me to the sort of business she did and I would later set up on my own. She had assured me that I did not particularly need an education to be a supply contractor. There were many women, as I would soon find out, who were stark illiterates but were doing very well as supply contractors. This, I later found to be quite correct.

For a start, I accompanied Maybel on her various trips through government departments and the offices of the big trading firms in Port Harcourt. We met all those who were in a position to give her supply contracts. They all knew her very well and had transacted business with her in the past. So it was a question of her checking on new opportunities that might have arisen or getting paid for work that she had completed.

Invariably, as we entered an office, Maybel would exchange greetings with the official, who was always male, then she would introduce me as her 'sister by the name of Lemona'.

'Good morning, Lemona.'

'Good morning, sir,' I would answer.

'Maybel, that's a right beautiful sister you have. A beauty queen if you ask me.'

'Don't look at her with lustful eyes,' Maybel would say.

'Oh no. It's not lust, but love. Am I free to love her?'

'No, I'm sorry, you may be free, but she's not. She belongs to me,' Maybel would answer, and they would laugh.

On occasion, we would be invited to lunch at the club or in some restaurant with one or two of the men. Sometimes, at the end of the day, someone whom we had met in the course of our journey through the offices would stop by at the house and be treated to drinks, or he would arrive with a friend and the four of us would go out to a party, to dinner, or for a quiet drink in some private house or a company guest flat.

I was not the only one in Maybel's outfit. There was Uche and there were a lot of others whom I met over time. It took me quite a long time to realize that Maybel was trading with us. We were all young, came from poor backgrounds and were anxious to do well in a town we knew little about. Maybel's ploy was to use us to obtain her supply contracts. The men were game. They had to satisfy their lust before they would award a contract to a woman. Maybel had most probably calculated that she could not possibly go to bed with all the men with whom she did business. Her answer was to keep a coterie, a bevy of pretty young girls whom she could use in baiting the men. That way, she did not have to pay as women contractors paid – a percentage of the value of the contract and their bodies into the bargain. In Maybel's case, she paid cash, but then the men paid Maybel's girls, as we came to be known. It was good business, and I suppose it worked for Maybel, profitably.

I was to learn from Uche and the others that when they first arrived in Port Harcourt, they had been guests of Maybel as I now was. Gradually, they had raised the funds or gained the friendship which saw them out of her flat into their own rooms or flats. They maintained contact with her, of course, because she continued to have new men to offer, and she knew a great number of people, including new arrivals in town or visitors. Invariably, in the latter case, they were men of either power or wealth, and were in need of entertainment, of relaxation, of fun. They were prepared to pay.

I slid innocently, if that is the right word, into Maybel's trap. Imagining that she was being kind, as Mama Bomboy had been, I accepted her advice and followed where she led until I had frequented all the bars and nightclubs of Port Harcourt, eaten in the best restaurants, and become used to alcohol. Before I met her, I had not had a drop of alcohol, but if I was offered a choice of drink in later days, I would settle for a whisky soda or gin and lime or a beer. And the more I drank, the more I lost the power to resist men's sexual advances. Sex became a routine, almost a daily routine. The men came either to the room I occupied in Maybel's flat or they took me out to a hotel or to some 'guesthouse' where clients paid by the hour, or to their homes when their wives were absent. Some even laid me in their offices. Most of the men found me completely irresistible. I was often amused at the way they virtually collapsed, trembling with excitement at the sight of my breasts, the way they exhausted themselves even before they had begun, and the way they would promise anything, if only they could please themselves with me. I was, in almost all cases, not emotionally involved with these men. Things were just happening to me which I expected to happen in my circumstance. Nor did I do it for money. I suppose it was Maybel's tutelage that did it. I offered myself and the men, impressed by my looks and by the fact that I was not bargaining like a trader, paid and paid handsomely. Of course, Maybel ensured that they were men who could pay handsomely. And then offer her what she wanted – business, contracts. By the end of my first year's stay at Maybel's, I had become a 'bad girl', whichever way you choose to interpret that. I knew it and I was not making any apologies.

Nor did it stop there. There was another side to Maybel which I was not aware of initially. It took me quite some time to realize that all the men who came to her flat never did spend time with her. They sat and chatted with us in the lounge and ended up in the guest room, with me. Even when we were a foursome and went dancing or to dinner, her guest was always the one to end up sexually disappointed. I felt like asking why that was the case, but dared not.

The answer came one night when we were together. We had

had a long day doing the rounds of the offices and had returned home to prepare and have dinner. We bathed in turns and sat in the lounge to chat. We were in our nightgowns. I began to yawn sleepily and decided to retire for the night. As I got into bed, Maybel joined me and before I could say a word, she had planted a kiss on my lips, much as any man would have done. Then she started to explore me and encouraged me to do the same to her. I was benumbed by shock initially, but seeing how excited she was by what she was doing, I obliged her until she dissolved in a frenzy and collapsed in a heap beside me and slept there all night. She was to repeat the same on several other occasions. I mentioned this experience to Uche confidentially at some point and she confessed to having had a similar experience with Maybel. And that explained why her men were always the ones to go home sexually frustrated. Maybel's appetite was not the usual one.

Two years or so after I had moved in with Maybel, I began to itch to leave her. By then, I knew my way about town thoroughly and had several friends and acquaintances of both sexes. There was no shortage of men who wanted me to be their mistress; who wanted to keep me to themselves exclusively. They would put me up in a furnished flat and provide me with a monthly allowance. Some offered me a car so long as I was at their beck and call. I resisted all offers for a while. I was young and wanted my freedom. I was not going to be tied down to any man unless that man wanted to marry me. Yes, I did think of marriage, in an oblique sort of way. But it was not important. Not at all. Not yet. I was having fun and getting money, which I invested in good clothes. My wardrobe was something to admire! I was virtually insatiable and exulted in those dresses no end. Eventually, though, I yielded to the pressures of Adoga, a general manager with the United Africa Company, whom I had met through Maybel. He was a tall, handsome man, old enough at forty-five to be my father. But he was kind, and would spend hours and hours with me, chatting and not necessarily wanting to go to bed with me. Whatever I wanted, he immediately provided. It was as though I mesmerized him. Indeed, I think I did. If you described him as my slave, you would not be mistaken.

I had been going out with him for three months when he offered me a furnished flat, and I accepted. He hired the flat, paid a year's rent in advance, furnished it completely to my taste, and it was time for me to move in.

One night, I mentioned the fact to Maybel. She flew into a jealous lover's fit. Why did I prefer Mr Adoga to her? What could he provide that she couldn't? She had brought me up from the market-place and introduced me to high society in Port Harcourt and now I was turning my back on her. Did I realize how much she loved me and wanted to care for me? Did I know that jilting her would cause her heartbreak? What did I want? She would give me anything. Anything. So long as I did not move out of her flat and into the flat which Adoga provided me and so be completely his woman.

I felt really sorry that night for Maybel. But my mind had been made up. I did not share Maybel's sexual preference. I wanted men and I had got one of the best in Adoga. I moved out of Maybel's flat and her life the next morning. I never did set eyes on her again after that day.

Funny the way people came into my life and disappeared, as if they were meant to lead me some of the way on my life's journey and do no more than hand me over to the next person in a sort of relay race.

CHAPTER SIX

The Mistress

The flat which Donatus Adoga rented for me was in a secluded area of the town, and he had personally selected it for the privacy it afforded him. I had chosen the furnishing for it myself and he paid every single penny it cost. He said it was his desire that I live in absolute comfort and that nothing should stand in the way of my pleasure. Besides, he wanted, whenever he was with me, to feel at home, to live at the level of luxury to which he was accustomed.

Donatus claimed to be a devout Catholic. He had been married in the Church almost twenty years earlier, and he and his wife had four children aged nine to nineteen. He was a very decent man, well-dressed, well-spoken and very much on the go. He held a good job – after all, the United Africa Company was the biggest firm in the country, and being general manager of one of its divisions was certainly an achievement. He told me that he expected to be managing director some day – perhaps the first African who would ever rise to that position.

The job mattered a lot to him and so did his family. Therefore, an affair, he stressed again and again, had to be kept absolutely private. To advance in his job, it was essential that he be a man of integrity who would never betray a confidence, a man who had no skeletons in his cupboard and who could not, therefore, be blackmailed. As far as his family was concerned, he owed a lot to his wife, whose connection with the Catholic Church had enabled him to advance in his profession. He would not be drawn on this, but let me know that his wife had never offended him and that he was loath to offend her in the slightest manner. She was a woman who would brook no disloyalty on his part and she was as jealous as —. They had lived the last twenty years like love-birds and he had not so much as had a passing liaison outside his marital home.

He had made every arrangement not only for my comfort, he told me, but also to ensure that I was not short of spending money. Apart from the monthly allowance which he would pay into my current account, he had also made arrangements with the manager of one of the trading companies (not his own employers) to appoint me a commission agent for their goods, particularly those that were in high demand. I would earn a commission on all such goods sold. Buyers were easily found. In this way, I would be in a position to earn a lot of money without much effort.

I moved into the flat with my suitcases. My wardrobe had grown so much that I now needed five suitcases. And I was content, surrounded as I was by all comforts, and with the assurance that funds would be available to me in a way I had never imagined or dreamed of.

I led a charmed, if not charming life, at the start. That first night in my flat was one I will always remember. The very feel of it! Donatus, or Don, as I called him, decided to make the night memorable. We went out to dinner at his favourite restaurant, then we stopped by a nightclub, where we danced to some high-life music before returning to the flat excited and flushed and going to bed – for a night of love.

No, not a night. After we had made love and I thought I would sleep in his arms, Don rested for a while, and rousing me from the sleep into which I had dissolved, informed me that he would be leaving.

'Why?' I asked sleepily, with a yawn.

'I have to get home.'

'But . . . but . . . it's our first night together in this flat.'

'I know. But I must get home. I have an early-morning appointment.'

'How early?'

'Very early.'

'You can leave here as early as you wish.'

'It's already one thirty and my appointment is for four thirty.'

'Oh, I see. Well then . . .'

'Take care, darling. I'll see you later today.' Don was already getting dressed.

'All right. I take it you're not travelling out of town.'

'No.'

'OK. I'll see you later. Good night.'

'Good night.'

'Leave my key on the dressing table. And lock the door before you leave. I'm too tired to see you off,' I said. Donatus kept one set of keys to the flat – to the front door and to every room, including the kitchen. This, he said, was to give him easy access to the flat whether I was there or not.

I was very excited about him at the time and since he treated me with the consideration a girl would expect from a father, I did not give a second thought to what he had proposed. Nor did I realize what a jealous lover Don was. He had given me some inkling when he told me that he wanted me for himself alone. I did not realize exactly what he meant, presuming that he was speaking as most of the men I had met often spoke.

The next night, Don turned up. I had prepared my first meals in the flat that day and it took all my time to get a good dinner going, with wine and all. I had learnt how to cook various meals at the Manas' and my time with Maybel had sharpened my skills, as I had had to do almost all the cooking for both of us. We had a candlelight dinner. I was really all happiness, and Don responded to me with the many anecdotes he had as a well-travelled man.

I had thought that he would spend the night with me. But shortly after dinner, which lasted a pretty long time because of the chat we were having, Don told me he would be leaving. He didn't even ask to make love to me.

'Another appointment?' I asked, teasing.

'No. Family,' he replied.

He always refrained from speaking about his family, particularly his wife, to me. I respected that, because I was likely to get jealous if he spoke about her. Indeed, I remember that once when he dared to mention Aduke (his wife), I threw a tantrum, most uncharacteristically. I don't believe he thought me capable of the anger I displayed on that occasion. After that, 'the family' became the code for his wife.

'I suppose I come a poor third after your job and family.'

'Why?'

'Because early this morning, it was an appointment, maybe a business appointment, and now it's the family.'

'Never mind, darling. We'll have lots of time together, now you have a place.'

'I hope so, Don.'

And he stood up and embraced me. He never kissed me on the lips. Said it was not African.

As I saw him downstairs, he said, 'By the way, I'm off on tour tomorrow. I'll be away for a week. I'll see you Wednesday week. Be good now. Don't do what I won't like.'

'A whole week.'

'Business, darling. Keep yourself busy.'

'I'll try. I'll miss you.'

'That makes two of us. Good night, baby.'

'Good night, Don.'

He got into his car and drove off into the night. I returned to the flat with mixed feelings, but I shook off my depression and got down to clearing the dinner table, doing the dishes and then settling down to listen to music on the radiogram.

The following week was a busy one for me, as I went about the shops and the market-place, linking goods with buyers. I found it quite interesting. One of the managers in one of the firms made passes at me as I sat with him negotiating the goods. He found every possible reason to keep me in his office, and I noticed that he hardly concentrated on what he was doing.

'Where d'you live?' he asked.

'Somewhere very far from here,' I parried.

'Am I allowed to visit?'

'No. My husband will beat you up,' I lied.

'You're married?'

'Yes.'

'But you don't have a ring on your finger.'

'I have it in my heart.'

'I think I'll take a chance and accept your husband's blows,' he said.

58

'Good luck to you.'

'You're a very beautiful lady. Your husband must be a very happy man.'

'Why?'

'Just looking at your face each time he returns home.'

'He could get bored with it.'

'I would never.'

'That's what you say now. Until you get accustomed to it.'

'Well, keep me in mind. In case you get bored with him. He can't be as handsome as I am.'

I laughed. 'He's a hundred times more handsome.'

I had learnt to be on an even level with men. The days were gone when I would have scowled and fretted at the sound of a man's banter, haughtily putting him off. Again, I think it was the time I spent with Maybel that sorted me out. Haughty and standoffish when I started out on my career ('career', did I say?), I soon learnt to be a good conversationalist and to accept and crack jokes and make men feel at ease.

I do not know if all my rough edges had been smoothed out, after all. I did not have a formal education; but I got on well with men. I was aware that my English was not perfect, but I was working at it, listening carefully to those with whom I spoke and imitating them. In any case, I could always revert to pidgin English if the going got rough.

During that same week, I met with Uche and Ngozi, another friend I had met during my time at Maybel's, in the market and invited them to my flat. We took a taxi there together and I watched with delight as they oohed and aahed about everything in the flat.

'Lem' (that's what they called me), 'you've really made it,' Uche said.

'Who's the man?' Ngozi asked.

'Donatus Adoga.'

'The UAC general manager?'

'That's him.'

'Ah, my dear, if I were you I'd grab him from his wife. She must be as old as your mother,' Uche asserted.

'He's very devoted to her,' I argued.

'Yes. Until you turn up and play your card. Only play your card right, that's all,' Ngozi said.

'He's too old for me,' I essayed.

Uche and Ngozi laughed and laughed long. 'Too old to be a husband, but not too old to be a lover! How about that?' Uche laughed again. 'And you're not too young to be his mistress, right?'

'What if a young man near my age should turn up?' I asked.

'He won't put you in a super furnished flat like this, give you a monthly allowance, introduce you to business, allow you plenty of time to yourself.'

There was something in that, I had to agree. 'But he'll love me and give me all his time.'

'Doesn't Mr Adoga love you?'

'He does. But time. Our first night here, he couldn't spend the entire night with me. And the next day, he pleaded family reasons and left after dinner. Then he informed me he'd be away for a whole week. I'm expecting him back tomorrow night.'

'How d'you know the young man you meet will give you all his time? Men are inconstant. I bet if he finds you attractive, you won't be the only girl he's found so attractive. He could go dancing,' Ngozi answered.

'And as to that age difference between you and Adoga, forget it. Our parents in the village married us off even before we saw our period. Or isn't that so where you come from?'

'It is,' I replied.

'So that's that. Is there food in this house?'

'Yes. I'll get something ready quickly.'

'We'll join you,' Ngozi said.

And we all invaded the kitchen and before long, we were having a meal with stout beer and all.

Uche and Ngozi left me late that night after wishing me luck in my 'palace'. They had to return to single-room apartments, the same as the one I had lived in when I was Mama Bomboy's ward.

The next night, Don returned as he had said. According to him, he drove straight from the airport to my flat. I welcomed him warmly. I was really happy to see him back and, although he appeared tired, he was quite warm and effusive towards me, loving and caring. He brought me several bottles of perfume.

'I'll prepare dinner. You must be tired.'

'No, darling. I'm not having dinner with you tonight.'

'Why not? You've been away for a week!'

'It's all right. There will be time enough. I'm not travelling for some time. I'll be in town for a few days.'

'A few days? You're not going off again so soon?'

'The demands of the job, dear. It's been like that all my working life. That's what it takes to be at the top ... er ... close to the top, if you like.'

'So what do I do with the dinner I prepared for both of us?'

'Keep mine in the oven. I'll have it tomorrow night.' Then he changed the topic, seeing that my face had changed. 'How did the business go?'

'Oh that. It's all right. I met a new boyfriend in one of the companies I visited.'

'You can't be serious.'

'I am. He's asked to visit me.'

'You're joking.'

'Maybe I'll share dinner with him since you don't want it.'

'All right. I'll have dinner,' Don agreed.

That's how I got him to sit with me at the table. But I observed that he merely nibbled at the food. And he had no sooner finished than he literally ran off.

I felt really frustrated, even angry, and could not eat any more. I cleaned the dining table and went to bed without doing the dishes. I lay tossing in my bed all night.

It was still early days in our relationship and I was yet to get used to Don's long absences and his short stays with me when he did eventually turn up. In those days, I did wonder if I could live with it all. Whenever he left me at night, it meant that I had to stay all alone. I felt ever so lonely! And I began to miss Maybel's place. At least there, I always had her to converse with, to cook with, to lunch and dine with. And we never lacked company, male or female. The way it was now, I always had to wait for Don. Be at his convenience.

No, that is not absolutely correct. For instance, the day after his return, we spent a long time together. He came from the office directly to my flat and took me out.

'Get ready, we're going out,' he said as soon as he arrived at the flat and I let him in.

'Where are we going to?'

'My secret. Just get dressed.'

I was excited. 'Wait for me then while I get myself fitted out,' I said.

'Your best dress, darling.'

'All right.'

I served him a drink, a whisky soda, and disappeared into the bathroom. By the time I got to the bedroom to dress he was there, lying across the bed in shirt and tie, having left his jacket in the lounge. He watched me dress.

'Hey, sweet, you look gorgeous without your clothes.'

'Maybe I should go out with you this way,' I teased.

'Yes. Come to think of it, I'd prefer that to your being decked out in those clothes which cover your lovely pointed breasts and perfectly formed pelvis.'

'I've heard that before.'

'From one of your numerous boyfriends? Don't tell me about them.'

'No, it was from a woman.'

'How did she know? You didn't undress before her, did you?'

'No. She was able to see beyond my clothes, which I imagine you cannot do,' I replied as I put on my clothes and make up.

I was not yet ready when Don got up and wrapped me in his arms, from behind my back.

'You mighty temptress,' he whispered into my ears. 'You're irresistible!' And his hands cupped my breasts, holding them hard, as he put his cheek next to mine.

'You're going to ruin my make-up,' I replied.

'Who cares? Come on, love, I need you.'

Before I knew a thing, he had begun to undress me. And after he had stripped me completely naked, he lifted me on to the bed, switched off the light and undressed.

Later, I got dressed again and we went off to his favourite restaurant for dinner. When we returned, he stayed with me for quite a long time, and it was well after midnight before he took off back to his family.

So long as he was in town, I had enough, I think, of his company, given his busy schedule. Of course, there were those frustrating occasions when he would tell me he was coming to dinner or just to be with me, but I'd never see him. I would sit and wait and wait and wait, parting the window blinds at the sound of a car passing by only to find that it was not him, and I would return to my seat disappointed and frustrated. Sometimes, I'd sit in the lounge waiting until I dropped off to sleep. And I would wake up in the morning feeling really bad.

I would feel, then, like going to his office to ask what had happened. But I was under orders not to drop in there, and I had to obey, in his interest. He was determined to keep our relationship as much under wraps as possible.

Occasionally, he took me with him on his many trips out of town, particularly if he was going to stay in his company's guest-house. I enjoyed such trips immensely, because they gave me the opportunity to see new places, and I could get away from Port Harcourt for a few days. Besides, I had him to myself at night, the whole night, which was so different from what happened in Port Harcourt when he always had to return to his family and could not spend the whole night with me.

For two years and more, all went well between us, or as well as could be expected in the circumstances. But in the third year of our relationship, he had to go abroad for three months on a training course. It was the first time we were going to be apart for such a long time and I think he sensed that I might not be able to bear the separation. Although I did not entertain any such fears and assured him that I would be waiting until his return, he did not appear to believe me. In the days before he travelled, he gave as much time as he could spare and we went dining out night after night. He made me promise to remain faithful to him, and I did.

In those months, I felt really lonely, and sought the company of Uche and Ngozi much more than I had ever done before. They and their friends came to visit me a lot more and we would sit and chat for hours. In time, my flat became a regular meeting point for young people, men and women my age. I found them quite interesting and their company very entertaining. For the first time, I was meeting young men of my own age. Uche and Ngozi gradually pressed me to go with them to parties where young people met one another, danced with one another and lived it up.

Again, it was a new life for me, if you see what I mean. Inevitably, I met a young man who liked me. Edoo Kabari. The initial attraction was that he came from a village close to Dukana and that, of the entire company we kept, he was the only one who could communicate with me in my mother tongue, a language I had not spoken since I arrived in Port Harcourt because I was not keeping company with people from Dukana. I was later to find out that he had just graduated from the University of Ibadan, was extremely funny and vivacious, and well-dressed. He was not handsome or elegant. He was squat, with the arms of a bear, and looked pugnacious. He was just a struggling young man. In keeping with the times, he had just taken delivery of a car on hire purchase and was still very excited about it. I guess he found me attractive, or in his own words, 'very serendipitous' and stuck to me like a leech. At parties, he could not take his eyes off me. He refused to dance with any of the other girls, insisting on always dancing with me. I did not encourage him at all but he would not let up.

I recall the first party at which we met. It was held in the flat of one of his friends, another young graduate. It was virtually bare of furniture. He had just moved in, and this was supposed to be a house-warming party, sort of. There were several girls, outnumbering the men. I think it was what they refer to as a cattle market. We sat drinking, and listening to high-life music, until our host dimmed the light and declared the floor open. He took Ngozi's arm and they started to dance, cutting graceful figures in the semi-darkness.

Edoo slipped from the other end of the room towards me. I had noticed while we were drinking in the full light that he had kept his eyes riveted on me.

'May I have a dance?' he asked, and pulled me up by the hand without ado.

I stood up. He tried to hold me close but I extricated myself and danced on my own. He came close to me, all the same, and began to speak to me, in the hum of the music on the radiogram.

'What's your name?' he asked.

'Yours first, if you please.'

'Sorry, I'm Edoo Kabari.'

'I'm Lemona.'

'Hey, that sounds familiar. Where d'you come from?'

'Dukana.'

'What do you know! You're my sister.'

'You come from Dukana as well?'

'No. I'm from Kibera. Next door to Dukana, kind of.'

'Yes. I've heard of it. Passed the road leading to it. Never been there.'

We fell to speaking Khana.

'What d'you do in town?'

'I'm a businesswoman.'

'What sort of business?'

'Commission agent.'

'Commission agent? What's that? Pardon my ignorance.'

'I'll tell you after the dance.'

The music came to an end and I returned to my place. The man whom I now knew as Edoo simply abandoned his place and came to sit on the arm of the settee. And that's where he sat for the rest of that evening.

Throughout the party, he nursed a single bottle of beer and he danced only with me, in spite of the fact that there were always girls who did not have partners. I did not dance with him all the time, though. I wanted to meet other young men.

It was a very lively party, and I enjoyed myself immensely. By the time we were done, in the wee hours of the morning, I was completely exhausted and part drunk. Edoo offered to take me home but I turned him down, choosing rather to be dropped off by Uche's boyfriend. I think Edoo was quite disappointed. But I thought that in my half-drunk state and with the way he was completely untouched by alcohol, he might take advantage of me. Besides, I had not had male company for some time, and I was, in truth, in need of it. However, I was sworn to fidelity to Don and was doing my level best to be loyal. And so I got home alone, tumbled into my bed and fell asleep in my party dress.

I did not see Edoo for another month or so. All that time, I kept looking forward to receiving a letter or a postcard from Don. But nothing arrived from him. I turned to my friends, Uche and Ngozi, and decided with them to host a party at my flat. We agreed that we were not going to allow the men to be the only ones who held a party and invited us to it. And this time, we were going to invite more men than girls so that the men would be the ones angling for dancing partners, the ones who sat down through the music.

I did not know how to get in touch with Edoo. However, he turned up on the night, invited by Uche's boyfriend. And once again, throughout the party, he made sure that he danced with me close throughout. It was a good party, noisy, with plenty to eat and drink. Uche, Ngozi and I had spent the whole afternoon preceding the party cooking. And we made food enough for all who turned up to have their fill and more.

It was while we were eating and drinking, before we started dancing, that I explained to Edoo, at his request, what a commission agent did. He listened to me patiently, expressing his surprise that I had come by such a profession at my age and had done so marvellously well as to afford the sort of flat I lived in. I did not tell him about Don. For all I knew, he might have known about him and was merely wanting confirmation of his information.

The party was as lively as the first one I had attended, and we danced till early the next morning. By about four o'clock, most of the crowd had gone, leaving Uche and her boyfriend, one other couple whom I did not know well, and Edoo and me. We danced until I could hardly stand and started yawning.

'Don't yawn,' Edoo said, 'it's still early days. I don't intend to leave until I've had breakfast!'

'Breakfast!' I asked in surprise.

'Yes. And he'll probably ask for lunch too,' Uche said. 'He's a chronic bachelor. Has no one to cook for him. No pots and pans in his house either.'

'Quite correct,' Edoo laughed. 'Maybe I should pair up with Lemona.'

'Sorry, mate,' Uche said. 'I think her hands are full.'

'Really?' asked Edoo.

'Absolutely,' I answered.

'Then why are you always alone at parties? I thought you didn't have a boyfriend.'

'Not with those looks,' Uche's boyfriend replied.

'Why's he so elusive?' Edoo queried.

'But you've only met Lem twice. That's not often enough time to judge. Besides, there's been one month in between the meetings.'

'No matter. I still think he's elusive. And I'll find myself a berth in the empty ship. After all, Lemona is a sister of mine.'

'Don't try your luck,' I said. 'You might end up with a broken nose.'

'Is he a boxer, then?' Edoo asked.

'Better than that, I assure you,' I replied.

And we all laughed. Edoo kept his word. He remained behind when everyone else had left, and I had to make breakfast, which we shared.

'You're a superb cook,' he said, as I made to clear the breakfast table.

'I'll be leaving now. I'll sleep the whole day. Be seeing you later this evening,' he said as he stood up to go. 'It's been a wonderful party. Thank you.'

'See you,' I said to him as he stepped out of the flat and made his way downstairs.

True to his word, he turned up later that evening with a number of friends, all male. They arrived each with a bottle of some drink or other and settled in after introducing themselves to me. They had come, they said, to gist. And gist, they did. For as long as ever. They sat chatting about everything under the sun while they sipped their drinks. Then, rather late that night, they bade me good night and departed in a group.

Gradually, my flat became the meeting point of this group of friends. Each of them felt comfortable dropping by in the evening or on a Sunday afternoon. But mostly it was Edoo who was always around. I did not mind his presence at all, indeed I welcomed it, because in Don's absence, I was really lonely, and if Edoo had not been there, I'd have felt bored. As it was, he helped ease my boredom, more so, as he was a good conversationalist. And we discussed lots of things, flipping from English into Khana mother tongue. I introduced Don to him *in absentia*, and once he knew I had a going relationship, did not ever make passes at me. He became a part of my flat, and I came to know everything about him. I was careful, though, not to reveal anything about my past to him. I was very jealous of my privacy and was not keen on letting anyone into it.

Thus did the three months of Don's absence pass. And the day of his expected return finally came. I was all expectation and prepared myself to welcome him back. I had to look my very best for him and I dreamt of him sweeping me off my feet into his arms. I forgot and forgave the fact that he had not written the whole three months he was away and invented excuses for him. I would ask him the reason, anyway, but would not make an issue of it.

I'd have loved to go to the airport to welcome him, but I had been told not to do so. That was the responsibility of his 'family'. And so I waited at home all day, counting the hours and waiting for the sound of passing cars, peeping through my curtained window or, on occasion, standing out on the balcony in full expectation.

He did not turn up all morning, nor did he show up all afternoon. Well, he might call in the evening. He did not. Nor did he come at night. Oh well, he would spend his first night after three months with his 'family' wouldn't he? I should, indeed, have known that. I was really expecting too much. And wasn't it a pity that I had no telephone at home? I'd at least have got a call, to let me know that he had returned at all. I lay tossing in bed at night, racked by all sorts of fears.

The next day was Sunday and I did not have to go out. I remained indoors, pottering around, pretending to be tidying up or at some work or other. However, all I did was wonder if Don had returned or not; why he had not called on me if he had returned; why he had not written to me during his absence. And then I fell to wondering if he had decided to break off our relationship.

I had told Edoo not to call on me that weekend as I expected that I would be busy. I began to regret that I had done so. All of a sudden, I felt how helpful he had been to me in starving off boredom by providing youthful company. And I wished he would call that Sunday.

He did, at about five o'clock. I was surprised to see him, but pleased, although I did not show it. Indeed, I pretended to be angry with him.

'Why have you come, in spite of my asking you not to?' I asked.

'I came to see your pretty, irresistible face, your serendipitous self.'

'But I told you I would not be available.'

'I know. Are you available or not? I can always take myself off. Has your man arrived?'

'That's none of your business. Do you mind?'

'Ah, that means he's not here yet. Didn't he return? Or he's still taking care of his wife.'

'You're meddling in my affairs, Edoo. I won't have it.' His words hit home.

'All right. We won't quarrel about it. After all, you're my sister. And I keep telling you, I'm available whenever you want me. Shall I go or stay?'

'Even if I ask you to go, you won't do so. What's the use? Sit down and have a drink. You're incorrigible.'

And Edoo spent the evening at my place, once again, filling the bored time with lively conversation. Was I grateful to him? By the time we were done, it was bedtime. When he left that evening, he embraced me and planted kisses on my cheeks for the first time. I did feel a thrill, a certain throb somewhere deep inside me. I put it down to a feeling of gratitude that he had taken away the anguish of my not seeing Don.

The next day, Monday, I busied myself with my business, using the opportunity to check discreetly if Don had returned from abroad. I found that he had. At least that was one doubt resolved. I thought that he would call that day, leastways. I made sure that I was home before five o'clock.

At eight o'clock that night, instead of Don, it was Edoo who called.

'Has he come yet?' he asked mischievously, a twinkle in his eye.

'No, if that helps you,' I answered.

'Never mind. Everything in its own time. God's time is the best.'

'You're in good humour this evening,' I said.

'Have you ever seen me depressed in your company? I've told you I'm nuts about you, and want you. You make me happy. Understand?'

'No, I don't.'

'So one man fails to turn up when he ought to. But the other man is at your feet. Why . . .'

'No, tempter. You're trying to ruin me. Look, Edoo, you're a friend. But I must ask you to leave. Please!'

'Why?'

'No, no. Don't ask. Just honour my wish, tonight. Please. Come back tomorrow, but leave me to myself tonight.' I began to cry.

'If you say so,' he replied simply. Then he passed his arms round my shoulders, gently, soothing, and said, 'Cheer up, baby. You'll be OK.' And he was gone. I looked at my watch. It was past eleven o'clock.

I heard him drive off. Soon after I heard steps on the staircase. What had happened? The door opened and in walked Don.

'Who was that who just left?'

'Welcome.'

'I asked who that was who just left?'

'A friend of mine.'

'It was late for him to be here.'

'Was it? Welcome, I said. You heard me.'

'Thank you.'

'You didn't have to start by bullying me, did you? You've been away for three months and three days. I didn't hear from you all that time . . .'

'So you thought it was all right to bring new lovers into my flat,' Don said.

I was stung by the accusation and could hold myself back only long enough to ask, 'When did you return?'

'Last Saturday.'

'And today is Monday.'

'Yes. I'm a busy man. I had a lot to tidy up after such a long journey.'

'And all the months you spent abroad? I didn't deserve a letter or a postcard?'

'I was up to my neck in work.'

'Truly? And you didn't give a single thought to the woman you left behind.'

'You had other company to keep you happy.'

That was it. 'You are a heartless, unfeeling man so full of your-self you do not care whatever happens to anyone else. You don't know what it is to sit here waiting on your pleasure. You don't know what it is, preparing dinners you will never eat. You don't know what it is, being left alone because the man in your life cannot spend the night with you. What haven't I borne for you? After all, you are old enough to be my father. Women my age who have men their age don't get treated so meanly. And why do you treat me this way? Because you hired me a furnished flat. So I'm not expected to speak to anyone else. I have to wait on you, wait for you, be at your beck and call, obey your every wish. And as if that wasn't enough, you start . . .'

I was still speaking when Don walked out on me and banged the door. I heard him drive away. I went into the bedroom and wept my eyes out. I could not fathom what had happened to him. This was a new Don altogether. What had I done? Or had someone been telling him tales of what I had been doing or not been doing? A myriad thoughts came coursing through my mind, jumbling things up. I was totally confused. Only sleep delivered me from torment.

The relationship between me and Don soured from that night. I did not see him for another week. And all that time, Edoo kept turning up, his friends too, so that my flat continued to be a place where young people met. I allowed Edoo to take me out on rides in his car and did not worry even if Don came to the flat and did not find me.

This last action had been recommended by Uche after I told her what was going on. 'He takes you for granted,' Uche said. 'Like most men, he's possessive and thinks you are cheap. Because he's rented you a flat, no one else can do the same? He's mistaken. With your face and figure, I know dozens of men who would fall over one another to please you. You can do whatever you like with men. Honest. Men are like kids. Make Don jealous and see if he won't come begging. On his proud knees.'

I doubted that, knowing Don for who he was. But I was determined not to be used and misused by him. In short, I was in rebellion.

Don did turn up after a fortnight. That evening, Edoo was at my place as usual, having a drink. When Don entered, I introduced the men to each other. Edoo shook hands with him and sat back. There was silence for some uncomfortable minutes. Edoo then tried to engage him in a conversation, but Don was brusque with him. I bit my lips as I thought how mean he was being to a man with whom I maintained an innocent friendship.

Edoo drank up and soon left, wishing me good night and promising he'd be back soon. He did not shake hands with Don. I saw him off to his car. When I returned to the flat, Don was fuming.

'Just what are you up to?' he asked, a frown creasing his brows.

'Just what are you up to?' I replied, in as spiteful a tone as I could muster.

'You can't abuse my goodness this way.'

'Can't I?'

'No.'

'Do your worst, then.'

'No, now, now, my darling girl, we can't go on like this.'

'Like how?' I demanded.

'Going at each other this way. We're supposed to be in love.'

'Are you?'

'Aren't you?'

'Don't give me that crap!' I shouted. I was a bit surprised at the level of my voice. 'You're looking for a slave, a sexpot. I'm not prepared to be either. If what riles you is that you rented this flat, I can always leave and find myself an alternative.' And the tears rolled down my cheeks. 'You are taking advantage of me!' I moaned.

That softened him, I believe. He came and took me in his arms.

'Leave me alone! Leave me alone!' I cried, and walked away from him. He came closer, apologized to me and led me to the bedroom. Before he left that night, he told me he needed privacy and was not willing to see those he referred to as 'strange characters' all over the flat whenever he came in.

Unfortunately, he had opened the sluice gates of rebellion. I began actively to seek alternative company, and particularly of males of my age bracket. I did not, of course, have to look very far. I went nightclubbing with Edoo and others. When Don found me absent on one or two occasions when he called, he cut off my monthly allowance. I did not worry about that. I was earning quite some money from the agency job he had arranged for me.

Once when he called, Edoo and two others were in my flat. He lost his temper and ordered them out. They refused to leave and laughed in his face. At this he called me into the bedroom and said ominously, 'Lemma, you are playing with fire. You know one side of me: the gentle and caring. But there is a darker, unforgiving side to me and when I call it into service, you and your new friends won't find it so funny.' And he stormed out. Edoo waylaid him in the lounge.

'What have you been telling her?' he asked.

'Get out of my way!' Don shouted angrily.

'Sugar-daddy, that's how you spoil young women. You should be ashamed of yourself.'

'Watch it, boy!'

When I heard the altercation, I dashed out of the room and ordered Edoo to get back to his seat. He obeyed me like a lamb.

73

Don went off, his face set, a picture of turmoil and wrath all bundled into one.

Inevitably, my affair with Don was heading down the precipice and was due for a great crash. Edoo and I had got quite hot for each other and I was not hiding the fact any more. We made love in my flat, in his. We went to parties together. He took me away on weekends to Onitsha and Enugu. He offered to take me to Dukana but I refused the offer. I had nothing to return to there. And the deeper I got involved with him, the more jealous Don became.

I found myself being trailed by Don. He had the spare key to the flat and he would let himself in in my absence and leave angry notes. If he found me in, he would swear his love to me, go down on his knees, appeal to me to return to the way I was with him, apologize for whatever he had done wrong. And if he found that I did not yield wholeheartedly and make him the promise he wanted, he'd go into a tantrum and promise to lynch me and my young lover. I think he could not forgive Edoo for calling him a 'sugar-daddy'. I wonder that he did not realize that that was also an insult to me. I never did really matter to Don, I found. I was useful as relaxation. No, I did not care for the life of a mistress. I did not want to be his mistress, his plaything, his bed of pleasure. I needed a life of my own. I needed to find my own man. I thought Edoo might fit the bill.

As fate would have it, Edoo and I returned one night from a party, fairly drunk, and we moved into the bedroom without locking the doors. Don came in and found us making love, and all hell broke loose. They went at each other, Edoo in the nude. I ran out of the bedroom and locked myself into the bathroom. I threw a bathrobe over myself and waited there trembling while the two men bloodied each other. I was entirely helpless and cried and cried, hoping to God that nothing would happen to either of them. By the time they were done, the lounge and bedroom were a sorry sight. There was blood all over the place, I found, when I finally crept out of the bathroom. Both of them were gone. I was left to clean up the aftermath of the fight.

The next day, what I had feared, happened. I got news that

Edoo had been involved in a fatal car crash. I was still in trauma that evening when three toughs barged into my flat. They were roughly dressed and had bloodshot eyes. 'We have orders to move you out of the flat,' one of them said gruffly.

I understood what they meant. 'I'll pack,' I offered.

'Quickly. We don't have time to waste.' And they laughed. One of them went to the fridge and got all the drinks out, ranged them on the centre table in the lounge, and they all began to drink, opening the beer bottles with their teeth.

I was scared to the marrow. I had barely enough presence of mind to throw all my clothes into my suitcases and to start carrying them downstairs. One of the men helped me carry them all out. My life as Don's mistress had ended.

CHAPTER SEVEN

Lover

I stood in front of the house, badly shaken, disconsolate and confused. I did not know what to do next. Had Edoo been alive, I'd
have headed for his flat. I thought of Uche and Ngozi. But they
lived in single rooms and I had too many suitcases. Should I return
to Maybel's? I hadn't seen her for a couple of years or so. And
she probably would not have forgiven me for the way I abandoned
her.

The night was thick and gloomy. There were no street lights in
the whole of Port Harcourt. I could only see the way from the
lights in the surrounding homes. The sky was a load of clouds,
hanging in moving bunches. A sudden gusty wind broke forth,
wild and angry, sweeping all before it noisily, shaking open
windows and lifting dust into my eyes. I covered my face and eyes
with the loose end of my head-tie. Then, the skies went on the
rampage. Click, crack, boom! Thunder. A dividing line shot across
the sky at the speed of light. Lightning. Then the skies opened
wide their doors and let out the clouds. Rain came pouring down,
first in heavy drops, and then in a flood.

Just in the nick of time, when I had begun to despair of finding
help, a taxi came by and I took it, asking it to go to the first place
that came to my mind: COMFORT GUEST-HOUSE, the scene of
many of my outings in those days when I lived with Maybel and
served her business partners for their common purposes.

We drove there in the blinding rain, through the flooded streets,
with thunder and lightning beating a frightening tattoo of terror.
I finally arrived at my destination, paid off the taxi and got a room,
where I took my suitcases. I was all wet and soggy, almost like a
sponge. I changed clothes and went to bed.

I have never been so miserable in all my life. I lay tossing about in the bed, assailed by a thousand thoughts which led nowhere. The difference between my flat and the room I was now bedded in was too stark. Depressing. But even more depressing was the thought that Edoo was dead. Car crash. I saw a link between that crash and my being thrown out of my flat. Donatus Adoga. The man whose mistress I had been for two years and more. He was a cold-blooded murderer? If he could treat me the way he did after those years and all he used to swear to me, what could he not do to Edoo, who had insulted him, slept with his woman and fought with him? His pride, his status, would not allow him to permit the story to circulate. It would have blighted his future, stopped his advancement. And he could not send a note asking me to leave the flat? He had to throw me out ignominiously, using hired thugs? Well, maybe I had asked for it by the way I was carrying on with Edoo? But what else could I do? Sit there waiting for him to kick me around as he pleased? But Edoo. Oh Lord, why did it have to happen to him? Why? And just when I thought I had found the sort of man I would have loved to marry? Well, no. But the relationship was growing. It might have developed into something more meaningful. It might not have. But he was a delight to live with. And now, what? What would become of me? Once again, I was adrift. Just like I was after the death of Mother, when I arrived in Port Harcourt from Dukana, unsure what to do and where to go. This time I had to reach into my handbag for the pills that would drown my misery in sleep. The rain droned on.

I saw my dead mother in my dreams for the first time. She was weeping disconsolately and as I walked towards her, she walked backwards, away from me, all the while keeping her eyes on me. I kept calling, 'Mother! Mother!', as I tried to get to her. I woke with the call. It was daylight. I took some more pills and soon dropped off to sleep again.

I lost count of time, of days. I must have been in this state of shock for two or three days. I would wake, order some tea and bread from a nearby 'hotel and bar', and eat, take some more pills and fall asleep.

When I finally pulled myself together, I remembered my business appointments. I had, as a matter of urgency, to get to one of the trading houses to collect some goods which had just arrived from overseas. I dragged myself there only to meet the gentleman who had informed me, when I started at the agency, that he wanted me for himself, and with whom I had joked. This time, he was not in a merry mood. He gave me the bad news. My agency had been wound down! Donatus Adoga had obviously been at work, extracting his last pound of flesh. To assure myself that this was truly the case, I called on another trading company and received the same news. I might, I thought, have expected that. Donatus was mean, mean, mean! Like all men, I found myself saying. But I had to retract that. Edoo had not been mean to me. And were there not mean women too? Mrs Mana? Maybel? What fate was it that was tossing me up and down this way? One moment, my luck would run out. And then I would find luck again. Like a buoy, a yo-yo.

Distressed to the point of depression, I returned to Comfort Guest-House. I demanded the key at the reception hall only to be told that it was not there. My heart missed a beat. I went to the room and tried the door handle. The door was not locked. I entered the room and beheld a sight that made me scream. All my suitcases had been rifled and every single article of clothing removed. The only item left behind was the knife I had taken from Mother's house after her death. I collapsed on the bed, screaming.

My screams must have drawn the guest-house staff and others to my room. They calmed me a little, and I blurted out the story between my sobs and tears. Nobody seemed to know what had happened. I grabbed the little knife, put it in my handbag, tottered out of the room in search of a taxi and headed for the nearest police station.

I was in a total daze. Standing before the desk sergeant at the police station, I felt like a sleepwalker in a maze. I must have mouthed something about my goods having been stolen from my room at Comfort guest-house. I thought I saw the sergeant writing something down – 'making a note', as they call it. And I must have heard him say he would come to investigate or send someone to do so. I found my way out of the station.

Now, where would I go to? What would I do with myself? I

stood by the road, waiting. A few cars and buses passed by, their headlights picking me out as I stood there, my handbag on my shoulders. I must have looked like some lady of the night.

A car pulling out of the police station I had just left stopped next to me and its driver asked if I needed a lift. Without answering, I opened the door and dumped myself on the passenger seat and began to weep uncontrollably.

'Where are you going to?' the man asked me.

'Nowhere,' I replied honestly, if foolishly. And I wept and moaned.

'What happened to you?'

'All my property has been stolen. All that I have in life.'

'Where do you live?' he asked.

'Nowhere,' I replied again.

He must have been shocked. And when, in later years, I thought of the incident, I often laughed at myself. But at that time, it was no laughing matter. I was traumatized. The death of Edoo, the loss of my flat, my business, my possessions, all coming on top of each other within the same week, or shall I say, within days of one another, would have driven me mad.

The white man in the strange car was the one who saved me. Yes, he was a white man. At the time, he spoke to me, it did not make a difference to me. He was merely a voice and remained so until we arrived at his house. He opened the car door for me after switching off the engine and getting out his side. I tumbled out of the car and was about to collapse, when he passed his arm around me and carried me in his powerful arms to the settee in the sitting room, and laid me there.

I faintly heard him call, 'Johnson!', and a man turned up on the instant. 'Let's have some tea. Quickly, please.'

And then I heard, 'How d'you like your tea? With milk and sugar?'

I nodded, I believe. He sat me up, put a cushion beneath my head and put the teacup to my lips. I drank up the tea and felt slightly better. I slid back into a lying position on the settee.

'Would you like something to eat?'

I shook my head. I indicated that I wanted to sleep. I heard his footsteps on the stairs, up and back. He slipped some pills into my mouth, and said to Johnson, 'Prepare the guest room for madam, please.'

I found myself, in the morning, in clean, scented sheets, in a wide bed, in an airy room in the Government Reservation Area, quite close to where I had lived eight or nine years back with the Manas. In that twilight state between sleep and wakefulness, I forgot my predicament until the memory of what had happened came flooding into my jaded mind. And my tears poured down like the rains of May, soaking the sheet which my benefactor had kindly provided.

I lay in a stupor in bed all that day. Even when my benefactor came into the room, I did not so much as get up. He said he came to find out how I was getting on, and was sorry if he had woken me from my sleep. He said Johnson would offer me breakfast and that he would see me upon his return from the office later in the day. 'Cheer up,' he said and shut the door behind him as he left.

I returned to sleep, and it was well after twelve o'clock when I woke up. I felt hungry. I had not eaten, I recalled, for over twenty-four hours. I sat up in bed, then got up and drew the curtains to let in the sunlight. It was a brilliant afternoon and the sun was in full glow.

A knock on the door brought in Johnson. He had obviously been waiting for me to wake up. He gave me a new towel and soap and showed me the bathroom. By the time I had had a shower and returned to the room, he came to announce that breakfast was ready. Would I have it in my room or in the dining room? I chose to go to the dining room. It would afford me the opportunity to move around a bit and possibly fix my mind on things other than my personal problems.

I did not find the appetite for the meal, although it was quite well prepared. I nibbled at it, had a cup of coffee and returned upstairs and fell into the bed. However, I could no longer sleep. I tried to put together the events of the previous day. What passed through my mind was that the same hand behind my ejection from the flat was also responsible for the burglary which deprived me of most of my earthly possessions. But for a small sum of money in my bank account, I was now as good as when I left Dukana to become a nanny at the Manas'. The mere thought of it brought hot tears coursing down my cheeks.

I was still weeping copiously when my benefactor returned. He was shocked to find me still weeping.

'Oh dear, oh dear,' says he, 'we're still weeping. Just what's the matter?'

The words came to my lips and died there.

'Now, let's see what I've got here. I imagine you don't have a change of underwear. So I got you some. Hope they fit.' He gave me a shopping bag. 'Whatever the matter may be, tears won't help you. So shall we dry them?' He brought out his handkercheif and wiped the tears from my face.

'I'm John Smith,' he said. 'I come from Scotland. I'm head of the Public Works Department. An engineer.'

I pulled myself together with some difficulty. 'My name is Lemona,' I said.

'Ah, I see. So we'll call you Mona. Mona Lisa. Ever heard of her?'

'No,' I replied truthfully.

'Well, she was a very beautiful woman. A famous painter drew her long, long ago. A pretty painting, famous throughout the world. There's a copy of the painting in the lounge. Would you like to see it?'

'Yes. But I need to change my underwear.'

'Fine. Take your time. Join me downstairs when you're ready. I'll be waiting.' And he left the room.

I changed my underwear for the new ones John had just bought me. They fitted perfectly. I was pleased. I went downstairs to meet John.

He was standing in front of the painting of Mona Lisa. As soon as I entered the lounge, he beckoned to me, 'Come this way. Here's the painting of Mona Lisa I was talking about. There has been a lot of argument about this painting. Some say there was actually a woman called Mona Lisa. Others argue that there was no such woman. That the painter, a famous Italian called Leonardo da

Vinci, merely imagined her. And the way he painted her, she looks enigmatic – I mean, you cannot tell, by looking at the painting, whether she was happy or sad. But of her beauty, there's no doubt. Everyone agrees that she was, is, very beautiful. Do you agree?'

'I think she is beautiful, very beautiful.'

'Is she happy?'

'Ehm . . . ehm . . . I don't think so.'

'Beauty does not bring happiness, then?'

'Not at all.'

'I understand how you feel . . . Now, to make this painting, Leonardo would have brought out his easel, sat Mona Lisa on a high stool, looked at her and sketched her on paper or canvas. Shall I show you how he did it?'

'Yes.'

John brought out his easel and put drawing paper on the board. 'Now, Mona, please sit down on the chair over there, and look at me.'

I obeyed him and he began to sketch. In less than twenty minutes, he showed me what he had done. It was like magic.

'Like that?' he asked as he held up the drawing paper on which he had sketched me in pencil.

'Yes,' I said, drawing nearer to see. It *was* like magic.

'Looks like you?'

'Very much.'

'Happy or sad?'

'I don't know.'

'Anyway, that's the sort of thing Leonardo did for Mona Lisa, and made her famous for ever. What about you? Who's been making you sad?'

'Oh, that. I've lost everything in one week. My business, my flat, my friends, my clothes.'

'Was there a fire or something?' John asked, consternation in his voice.

'Worse than that. I lost everything, everything. I'm alone and helpless.' And I began to sob again. I just couldn't hold back the tears.

'All right, Mona.' He held out his handkerchief again. 'All right.

Don't tell me the story now. I'll hear about it later. I'll see what I can do to help out. You'll be all right.'

'It's very kind of you to say that,' I said.

'I'll do my best,' he replied simply. 'Come, let's take a talk in the garden. It's a riot of colours at this time, and after the heavy rains of the past few days, the trees and shrubs must be in profusion, in fine leaf.'

He led me to the garden and introduced me to different flowers and shrubs, telling me their English names, and different things about each of them. The house was set in a large space which John had carefully turned into lawns, garden and orchard. I could see that he was a keen gardener in addition to being a painter and engineer. Maybe, he's other things too, I thought to myself.

It was getting late when we finished touring the garden and orchard. As we turned into the house, John suddenly stopped, held me gently by the upper arm, indicating that I halt for a moment. We were near a shrub with white flowers.

'Smell that!' he said as he plucked a branch of the flowers and gave it to me.

'Wonderful!' I said, sniffing fragrant flowers.

'Queen of the night,' he said. 'Most wonderful of flowers. All green and innocent in the day, but when night comes, it opens up, letting forth this amazing aroma, quite apart from its bushy, cream buds.'

'Ah,' I said, sniffing away.

'I think dinner is served. Join me. Johnson tells me you've not eaten all day.'

'I don't feel like it.'

'Feel better now?'

'Just a little.'

'Good. So you'll have dinner with me?'

'Thank you, John.'

'You're the queen of the night. Shut in the daytime, open at night. Redolent, pleasant, giving joy to the lucky ones who meet you.'

'No, it hasn't been so.'

'It should be so. You are, shall I say, the most beautiful woman I've ever met during my ten-year stay in Nigeria.'

I blushed.

'Your names always have meanings. What does Lemona mean?'

'Happy encounter, lucky meeting, something like that.'

'Well then, I hope ours will be a happy encounter, a lucky meeting, a fortunate event.'

'Amen,' I replied. I smiled to think of the interpretations he put on our meeting. It was not a meeting. He had saved me from death yesternight. Without him, I should certainly have died of heartbreak and trauma. Nor was the danger gone. As we sat down to dinner, I thought of the many things that could happen once I was out of John's place. I would only stay until I was well enough. But then where would I go?

John was silent all through dinner. I suppose he was responding to me as I sat and ate quietly, thinking to myself, with myself. My head began to throb painfully. I obtained permission from John to return to my room.

I was delirious for well on a month. A doctor came to see me regularly and it took me time to come round. Even after I did so, the doctor still recommended bedrest. It was during this period that I came to appreciate the goodness of John's heart, his kindness towards me.

I had never had anything to do with a white man in all my life. Even in those wild days when I was at Maybel's and we frequented bars and nightclubs where we met white sailors and business executives or oil-company operatives who were just beginning to come to work in Port Harcourt, I always stayed away from white men. I did not relate to them at all. I did not consider them as possible partners, sexual or otherwise. In my circle, it was thought that associating with a white man was the very nadir of prostitution. You couldn't even pretend that the white man was going to marry you. He would not take you back to his home. He was out to enjoy himself and everyone would know that. So if you were going out with him, it would be known exactly why you were doing it. Besides, white men were never circumcised. They'd look really funny in the nude with their pancake bottoms. And what of those long beaks they carried on their faces? And they had a way of handing over women to dogs to mate with. The woman would bark like a dog after that. It had actually happened to one girl. We worked out our prejudices this way. The fact, of course, was that none of us had ever come close enough to a white man. We even ostracized those girls who did, and therefore found it difficult to understand, appreciate, or know the white man as friend, lover or sexual partner, or even as a human being.

The Eastern Region of Nigeria, which included Port Harcourt, was now self-governing and there was noise of independence, Nigerian independence, in the air. None of that interested me. It had nothing to do with me or my friends. We never discussed it. But we did hear that the white men who had ruled us for so long would soon be going back to their home, and our own people would take over and do what the whites were doing for us. We would now be ruling ourselves. It was said that our own people would do such things better because they understood their brothers better. A famous politician went round and taught a song which became very popular: 'Everywhere there must be freedom. Freedom! Freedom! Everywhere there must be freedom!!!'

The fact of independence came to me as I lay recuperating from my illness. John, my benefactor, would soon be leaving and someone else would do his job. I kept that at the back of my mind. But before me was the extraordinary care he took of me while I was ill. He would sit by me, holding my hand and saying soothing words. He even told me stories of the many people and events he had encountered during his ten-year sojourn in the country. He had arrived as a twenty-four-year-old, after leaving university. Enrolled in the colonial service, he had been happy to be sent to Africa to work in the Public Works Department. He had read a lot about Africa, things which were quite uncomplimentary. But at the university, he had met two law students, one male and one female, both from Nigeria, and had struck up a friendship with them. He had found them very interesting, very polite, cultured and outgoing. They had given a different impression of their homeland, had excited his curiosity, and made him determined to join the British colonial service upon graduation and hope to be posted to Nigeria. His dreams had come true and he had spent ten years working in different parts of the country. He liked it a great deal and would like to live in it for the rest of his life.

He was a tall, gangly fellow, almost six feet tall, decidedly ugly, with long arms and long legs. He wore his hair short, his lips were thin, and he had a flat backside. His chest was very hairy, as were his arms and legs. A sallow-faced man with bulging eyes and a long beak of a nose, he looked repulsive from a distance. However, when he spoke, he exuded gentility in a soothing, deep voice. His hands were extraordinarily soft and supple.

Because of the way we met, it was not any of these physical attributes that impressed themselves on my mind. He was always going to be the storyteller, the painter, the man who knew everything about flowers and the possessor of a heart of gold, who had shown me great kindness when it mattered most. The picture of him, seated on my bed, holding my palm when I opened my eyes, is one that has stuck indelibly in my memory.

When I finally came through my illness, there was no question but that a relationship had sprung up between us. I liked him immensely, and I was later to fall deeply in love with him. He was the only man I had loved in my life, and that in spite of the fact that I had had liaisons with dozens of men.

He quickly made the memory of Mana, Maybel, Edoo and Donatus Adoga fade. He did not even ask about my past beyond wanting to know where I was born, what formal education I had, who my parents were and such. But he was so intelligent, he would have pieced the rest of my story together from what I said during our numerous conversations. I was not forthcoming at all on my relationships before I met John. That was my secret. It was to John's eternal credit that he never sought directly to know more than I was prepared to tell him.

We shared a beautiful life. He taught me how to drive, and he improved my knowledge of the English tongue. He would take me out to Port Harcourt Club to watch him play tennis; then later, he introduced me to the game and taught me how to play. We would go to the court early in the morning and play for an hour before returning home for breakfast. Then he would be gone to the office, leaving me to read books which he recommended, or to busy myself with Johnson, the steward, on household matters, or the gardener.

He also taught me how to drive. Within six months, I was the proud possessor of a driving licence and was cruising around in John's car. John played the piano well and there was an old one in the house. He tried to teach me how to play it but I was not interested. I didn't mind watching him play and possibly enjoying what he played (I didn't like a lot of it), but I just did not care for the instrument. I didn't have to like everything which John liked.

Our backgrounds could not have been more different. He was the second of two brothers in what he called a 'middle-class' family. I did not understand what that meant. Anyway, his father had wanted John to be a lawyer like himself and when John opted to study engineering, he was disappointed. He was even more distressed when John decided to go into the colonial service and was sent to Nigeria. The old man felt his son was a let-down and he disinherited him. John did not care what his father did or said. He wanted to lead his own life and it was probably the fact that he had nothing to return to in Scotland that made him decide to make Nigeria his home. Both parents had died within a year of each other five years after he had arrived in Nigeria. He had not heard from or written to his father ever since he finished his final exams at the university, and news of his death did not get to him until six months afterwards, by which time his mother was also on her deathbed, suffering from terminal cancer, he was told.

Besides the death of his father, he also spoke briefly about a love affair he had at university. It would appear that the girl had jilted him and married one of their lecturers, who was old enough to be her father. He never did, and never would talk about this aspect of his life at any length.

I did wonder if he had lost his manhood. Because for the first five months of my living with him, he did not show any sign that he desired intimacy with me. I had heard of men who only made love to men – like Maybel only made love to women. I asked myself again and again whether John was one of such men.

I got an answer one night, when we returned from an outing. We had had dinner at the club and then gone on to a nightclub where we listened to high-life music, which he enjoyed, although he did not dance to it. We had quite a lot to drink. As we drove back home, John and I were a bit high. He passed his arm around me even as he drove. By the time we got home, he stopped the car, planted a full kiss on my lips and as we got out of the car, he wrapped his arm around me. He led me upstairs into his bedroom. At that time, we were not sharing the same bedroom. There, without asking any questions, he kissed me while his hands busied themselves with my dress. He was quite clumsy about it. To save him the frustration, I broke loose from him and quickly undressed, while he did the same. He lifted me into the bed, planted kisses all over me – on my forehead, my eyes, my breasts, my navel, my thighs, my feet. Then, sucking my right breast while his right hand squeezed my left nipple, he went into me, gently, and then thrust away with all his might.

My body responded to him as it had not done to any other man. It was as though the months of waiting, of expectation, had stored in me a desire that was like a fruit, ripe and only waiting to be plucked, broken and sucked. I cried with joy and ecstasy at the pain, at the surging waves rushing to the shore, there to break with a headlong force. And then, spent and exhausted, we lay back panting. For the first time in my life, I had experienced an orgasm.

As I lay in his long arms, I experienced a feeling I had never known. And I did wonder that in all those years of my frolicking with a large number of men, I had never had that wonderful experience, that ecstatic moment.

Later that night and early in the morning, I sailed the same sea again. Each time, I clasped John to myself as though I would never, ever let him go.

That morning, the sun stretched forth its golden arms and fingers from the eastern skies through my soul, opening in my garden the petals of a beautiful flower in spangling colours. And gratitude radiated from my heart through to my eyes. John would have to be my man for ever. He and no one else. He, who had made me a woman. A woman! I could dance. I danced, I glowed, I exulted. I told John what he had done for me. All he said was, 'I'm happy for you.'

A new chapter in the book of our life had opened. And we wrote and read it together, with joy and satisfaction. We shared, and hoped that it would never end. We made promises to each other. I thought I had, at last, boxed the jinx that had followed me, making my life a misery. I hoped and prayed that all would be well now.

And so it seemed. One summer, when we had been together two years or so, John went back to Scotland on his first holiday since he arrived in Nigeria. He had always spent his holidays driving to different African countries. In our time together, we had holidayed in the Cameroons, climbing the Cameroon mountains and swimming in the sea at Victoria. The second holiday we spent in the cool of the plateau in Jos. He had told me that he did not fancy going back home to live in a caravan.

But that year, it began to be said that all expatriates who so desired could claim a large compensation and take an early retirement. Initially, John had shown no interest in it. He did not want to leave the service early, he said. Besides, he had a love for, a commitment to the country.

However, discussion with some of his colleagues and peers appeared to change his mind. The sort of compensation that was being spoken about could surely help one set up a new life in Britain? Why potter around in Nigeria when, with that sort of money in the bank as security, one could also look for other employment? One could take a mortgage on a house and be able to pay the instalments comfortably. It was probably too good an opportunity to be missed.

'I've been away from Britain for a long time. I doubt that I could live there again.'

'Of course, you can,' I said. 'It's your home.'

'It was. Ten years. A lot must have changed. I'll have to find out if I can survive there. If I'll like it.'

'A good idea.'

'I won't be away for long. One month should be enough for me. I can renew acquaintances with my elder brother too. I understand he's a successful doctor.'

'Yes?'

'He was destined for great things, was Paul.'

John began to speak excitedly about Scotland, its mountains, its scenery, its dances, and whatnot. It was as though he were reliving his boyhood once again. He did not include me in the plans which he discussed with me. I imagined that would come later. All the same, I did ask him how he thought I might get on there.

'Oh, that should be no trouble.'

'But I understand black people are not welcome there.'

'Of course they are. I've told you about my friends, the senior magistrate and his wife who's also a senior magistrate, Mr and Mrs Bankole. Excellent couple. They were popular on the university campus.'

'One or two individuals on their own merit. That does not mean that all black people are welcome.'

'You're correct, come to think of it. There's a lot of bigotry around. But it's not only aimed at blacks. The Jews, for instance. They suffer discrimination, as do the Irish.'

'But not as much as black people.'

'No.'

'You are British and you've spent ten years here among black people. Have you found out the reason why whites hate blacks?'

'I wouldn't put it that way. There's a lot of misunderstanding and bigotry in the world. Do not black people dislike each other?'

'Not because they are black,' I replied.

'But because they do not speak the same language, are not from the same tribes? Frankly, the subject is very complicated. One needs to write books on it.'

'And when whites marry blacks what happens?'

'They live for each other.'

'Are they welcome in Britain?'

'They would, of course, be odd, there as here.'

'Are their children accepted over there?'

'I don't have enough experience in the matter. But I should imagine they would have problems there as here. Because they do not really fit into a particular category.'

I left the matter floating there. John cared for me, I knew. He had told me times without number that he loved me. He had never broached the question of marriage with me but we had been living together for two years and more. And I loved him deeply. Marriage to him would be the fulfilment of my life. I looked forward eagerly to the day he would ask for my hand in marriage.

I did not think this impossible. After all, we had gone all over the country together and we had been seen together throughout Port Harcourt. Our association had not raised any eyebrows as far as I knew. We had been well received by his friends and my friends, few as they were, were quite happy for me. Indeed, they thought me very fortunate to have found in John a lover, a friend and a teacher. The one thing I lacked, a good formal education, he did not appear to mind. In fact, he had helped me make up for it. I now spoke well and I read quite a lot too. For I had a lot of time on my hands since Johnson did most of the housework and I only played a supervisory role. How I hoped John would propose to me!

And wasn't it a shame that I could not ask him myself? Oh why have women to act coy in these matters? Why will not custom, society, allow us to express ourselves equally with men? Why will society look down on a woman who has several boyfriends but approve of a man who has several girlfriends? Why will a woman who goes out on her own to enjoy herself or goes to a cinema or a party earn the opprobrium of society whereas a man does not suffer any such strictures for doing the same thing? Women are created different? Is that it? As I asked myself these questions, Mama Bomboy came to my mind. I still remembered some of the things she told me that day in the market when she lamented the fate of women. How right she had been! What could I do now, about my situation? How I wished there was someone, an older woman, a mother, perhaps a father, with whom I could discuss my worries? But I was alone, all alone. And I felt bad.

The date of John's departure drew near and he finally left. I saw him off to the airport.

'My darling, Mona, it's hard to say goodbye, isn't it?' he said, holding my hand. I pressed his hand in reply.

'Fortunately for us, I won't be away for long. Twenty-eight days only.'

'That's long enough.'

'Take care of yourself. I'll write as soon as I get to London. And, of course, I'll be right back, on time.'

'I'll miss you badly,' I said.

'Me too.'

'Take care, darling.'

'Goodbye, Mona.'

'Goodbye, John.'

'I love you, sweet.'

'I love you too.'

And he walked off into the plane. I watched him go. He waved to me from the steps before the plane swallowed him. I waited till he was airborne before I turned away and drove home, quite disconsolate.

Twenty-eight days. I counted them studiously. I tried to fill in the days with activity but was not very successful. It was then and only then I realized how wrapped up in John's life I was. The friendship I had with Uche and Ngozi was not really working properly because I hardly gave it the time it deserved. I spent most of my time with John. And when he was away at the office, I thought mostly of him or did things that were related to him. The fact of my having no relations did not help either. It meant that John was all in all to me.

I had not imagined that, all of a sudden, I would be able to forswear nightclubs and parties. Yet, that is what happened, unless John took me out.

It was soon over, anyway. John's holiday finally came to an end. I heard from him twice – the first time on his arrival in London when he sent me a postcard and at the end of the first week when I received an airmail letter that was full of terms of endearment and reiterated how much I meant to him.

I was at the airport to welcome him back. I fell into his outstretched arms. He looked really fit and well rested. He had lost his tan and seemed whiter than I had ever seen him.

'You had a good holiday.'

'Beautiful!'

'The weather?' I had learnt always to ask the British about the weather first thing.

'Not as good as you've had it here.'

'Pity. And your doctor brother?'

'Paul? Oh, he's fine. Very fine. I spent a weekend with him at his place in London.'

'Thanks for the postcard. And the letter.'

'You received them?'

'Oh, yes. And right on time.'

'Ah. I had thought that I might arrive before them. Happens sometimes. The mail is so dreadfully slow within the country.'

'You look good.'

'Thanks, darling. I had a lot of rest, I suppose. You too.'

'I missed you,' I said, as I started the engine of the car and we headed towards town.

The drive from the airport to the house was a short one, the airport was now almost in the middle of an increasingly bustling town, growing with the expectation of oil treasures and the renewed strength of coming independence.

Absence makes the heart grow fonder, it's said. It tore my heart apart. John could not really discuss his holiday with me. I had never been to Britain and I would not have understood most of what he'd have told me. Moreover, he had not taught me about his home largely because it never entered into his calculations that he'd go back there.

That first night of his return was bliss for me. I dissolved the loneliness of the past month in his arms of love. I told him of the way I had occupied my time – doing nothing aside from counting the days and sighing for him.

For his part, there was just a hint less warmth than usual. He must have been very tired. He did not make love to me with as much gusto as before. I put it down to what he complained of as 'jet lag'.

We resumed our life where we had left it before his leaving. He returned to his task at the office. When I asked how he had found Scotland after a ten-year absence, he spoke excitedly about it. And he gave me the impression that he would be going back. The compensation being paid for the early termination of his service would be enough to set him up at home, and it was quite possible that as an engineer he would find another job at home, even if he had to obtain new training.

It gave me quite a jolt. More so as he did not drop a hint as to my going back with him. I began to be restless. In the years I had spent with him, I had not earned any money, depending entirely on the allowances he gave me. Nor did I have much of a wardrobe. He himself did not have many clothes, all of his earnings being saved towards the annual holiday, with a little put aside for a rainy day. I was much poorer than when I was with Donatus Adoga. I did not like the feeling. But I did not mention it to him.

The months slipped past. Five, six months. I began to notice a decreasing ardour in John. He seemed a bit restless in my company, his conversation coming in monosyllables. He appeared to be very busy in the office, spending much more time there than usual. And we did not go out together as much as we used to. We did not even play tennis together any more. It had been a daily routine for us. I asked, I complained; all he told me was that he was trying to put things in order prior to his retirement. And he had to prepare his Nigerian subordinates to take over from him.

'You are definitely leaving, John?' I asked him one night after dinner.

'Yes, Mona. Your people have to take over. Good for them, I think.'

I did not know if he was being sarcastic. Sarcasm was not in his nature, though.

I finally found the courage to ask the question which had been gnawing at my heart. 'What happens to me?'

'I've been meaning to talk to you about that,' he said. He took a sip of his coffee. And then followed an uncomfortable pause. He drummed nervously on the table, I waited, and when he was not forthcoming, I said, 'Yes?'

He moved from the dining table and asked me to come over to the settee. We sat next to each other. He took my hand in his. 'Mona, I've had three lovely years in your company. It's been a beautiful time. I believe I never gave you cause to doubt my boundless love for you?'

'No. You've been marvellous and I thank you. You saved my life, I should say.'

'You are a beautiful woman. You have a soul as beautiful as your face and figure. I'm happy I met you. It completed for me a life I have enjoyed here; gave me memories which I will always treasure. Unfortunately, the fact of Nigerian independence has introduced a new element into my life which I had not foreseen. The fact that I have to return to Scotland or England, to the UK, has also meant that I have to review my plans, make a new life, so to speak.'

He dropped my palm. I was beginning to feel a slight chill. My lips trembled. John continued to speak.

'I have wondered, in making those plans, if we could live together in the UK. I know that you would have no objection to it.'

'No,' I said rather eagerly.

'Nor would I. We have discussed this matter before. I made investigations during my leave. And I find that there would be nothing stopping us from living there as we have lived here. There would be the usual discomfort of neighbours and all that, but we would be living for ourselves, not for them. And I couldn't care less what they think.'

'Nor could I,' I stated.

'But then, something happened while I was in the UK.' He stood up and walked towards the window, close to where the picture of Mona Lisa hung. He coughed hesitantly. 'Now, what I'm going to say is going to hurt, but I'd better get it off my chest. I've been wanting to, for a long time, ever since my return from the UK, but couldn't bring myself to tell you.' He cleared his throat again. 'While I was in the UK, I met and fell in love with . . . Well, let's say she fell in love with me. She was excited by the romance of Africa, I think. Charlotte's her name. We agreed to get married and to settle in London. She's coming here at the end of next month. We'll marry here and return together to London.'

I was stunned. I could not believe my ears. John had dumped me for another woman. That's why he had been cold since his return from his holiday. I got up on the instant, ran unsteadily upstairs and instinctively began to pack my things into a suitcase.

I worked feverishly, without thought, driven by my anger and distress. In retrospect, I'm sure I did not know what I was doing. At the bottom of the suitcase, I found the sharp little knife which I had inherited from my mother. I put it in one corner of the suitcase.

As I worked, I heard John's footsteps on the stairs. He opened the door and said, 'Mona . . .' The sound of his voice brought the bile to my lips. Impatiently, I seized the knife and threw it at him, shouting, 'Leave me alone!' The next I knew, there was a shout and a thud on the floor. I looked on, petrified. There was blood on the floor. I went towards John, as he lay face down, groaning.

'Save me, Mona, save me!' I heard him say.

I looked closely and what I saw filled me with horror.

'Johnson! Johnson!' I called. I think he was clearing the dinner table. He came up straight away. 'Help me turn John round.' John was lying face downwards. Apparently, the knife I had thrown had hit him in the heart; he had fallen face downwards and the sharp point of the knife had gone into him. 'Send for the ambulance,' I said as I tried to extricate the knife from John's heart. But it was useless. Each tug at the knife only brought howls from him. I was splattered with blood. By the time the ambulance arrived, life was oozing out of John. We carried him downstairs and put him in the ambulance. But it was useless. John was dead, killed by me.

CHAPTER EIGHT

I have lived that scene again and again over the last twenty-seven years. My anger and despair at John's desertion, the confusion which led me to pack my things, even though I had nowhere to go and had no plans whatsoever to leave, the impulsive taking up of the knife, the way John's voice incensed me and made me throw the knife at him. And why on earth did it land on his chest with its sharp point? Then John had to fall forward and push it right through his gentle heart!

When I found out that John was dead, I simply fainted. When I came to, I was in hospital. I had to be heavily sedated for a week. And thereafter, I was taken into police custody.

Before anyone could condemn me, I had already condemned myself. I did not need anyone to tell me that what I had done was wrong. I did not care to think of the extenuating circumstances. John had been wonderful to me. He had given me three unforgettable years. When I threw the knife, I had not meant to kill him. It was the act of a moment of anger. And if he had not fallen on the knife, he would not have died. But those were ifs. The fact was that the man was dead. I had lost the best man I had ever met in my life, a man who had given me so much, including making me a woman, a sexually fulfilled woman. And in losing him, I had got lost myself.

No, I was not going to place myself at the mercy of cruel fate any more. No longer would I give fate an opportunity to play games with me. I had a death-wish. If I lived any longer, I would only get involved in further fatalities. Mine was an unlucky star. Maybe I had contributed to my misfortune. Maybe not. But I would accept all the blame. Had I not fainted when I did, I would have taken my life. Now all I wanted was for the court to sentence me to death. I would gladly die and join John wherever he was. I would, on meeting him, apologize to him and request his forgiveness. I had done wrong and my behaviour was truly inexcus-able. I begged the same forgiveness of Almighty God who, all-seeing, would know that I had meant no harm.

While I waited in police custody as investigations were made, I knew that I would be the hub of gossip and discussion in our circle. The police would dig into my past and come to the conclusion that I was a bad woman, a very bad woman, with an evil past. All those men with whom I had had liaisons in the days when I lived very much under the influence of Maybel would condemn me. Donatus Adoga would thank his stars that he had broken with me, otherwise I would have treated him the way I had treated John. They would invent all sorts of stories about my past and find justification for the conclusion they would have reached about me. There would be some who would allege that they always knew that a liaison between a white man and a black woman was unnatural and bound to end in tragedy. And they would blame John for picking me from the streets and for wanting to make a different person of me. I was so far below him. He ought to have found a black woman, if a black woman he needed, who had a more enlightened background. How, they would ask, had he found me? He must have been dazed by my great beauty. And wasn't I ambitious to think that he would have married me? I had even begun to dream dreams of going abroad with him. I would not have known that I was just there to satisfy his local pleasure. My example would teach both white and black in future to be wary of each other and not start to imagine the impossible in their relationships. And there would be those, especially in the white community, who would know that John had got engaged during his leave to Charlotte. They would tell the story to the police.

I doubted the extenuating circumstances would be considered. A black woman killing a white man in a place where the white man was ruler and king was very wrong. The ruler had to show that he had the power. That would probably work in my favour and bring about a quick trial.

In that, I was correct. Before long, I was before the magistrate's court for the preliminary inquiry. I did not hesitate to plead guilty. The magistrate seemed entirely taken with me. He stared at me endlessly and I could see, as a woman of some experience with men, that he was excited, lustfully excited. If only he knew that I was dead to the world! He advised that pleading guilty did not mean the case would not be as properly tried as if I had pleaded not guilty. That made no impression on me. He asked that I be remanded in prison custody. The state was to provide me with legal defence.

I was not interested in that, either. When the lawyer came to ask me questions, I told him not to bother. I had murdered John. Had dug my knife into him. The knife was mine, the hand that held it and turned it in his heart was mine. I was not going to say why I did it. The reasons were mine and mine alone. I would never tell them to anyone. He advised that if I had done it in error, that could earn me due mitigation. If I had done it in a moment of anger, and showed that my anger was justified, he could save me. Save me! No, I did not want to be saved. The man had been extraordinarily kind to me and I loved him. I had murdered him. He was dead; all I wanted to do was to join him wherever he was. Such was the extent of my love for him. But he had heard that the man had got engaged when he went on holiday. Had I murdered him because of that? Had he promised to marry me in the three years we had lived together? He had made no such promise and I was not aware that he had got engaged while abroad. So why had I murdered him? I alone knew the reason. The lawyer was very frustrated. He shook his head sadly and left me.

The case eventually went to the High Court and after several adjournments, and questionings to which I gave half-hearted answers, I listened to the prosecution describe me as a woman of low character, poor background and even poorer upbringing, who traded my great beauty and sex for unwarranted advancement. I had a record of unimaginable sluttishness; a lady of the night, I was always to be found in the cheapest, meanest whore-houses. I had no feelings whatsoever for any man; I was a grabber. Money was the motive power of my life and I would do anything to get it. Although I did not have a history of violence, I was always within inches of it, and certainly what I had done to John Smith was to be expected. The fact was that I had hoped he would marry me and take me away to the United Kingdom. Once I found that that dream was not realizable, my decision was to kill the unfortunate man. And I had set about it in calculated style, waiting for a moment when we were in our bedroom and he had no chance of escape to dig into him with a knife I had bought and specially prepared for the purpose. He was asking for the death penalty to serve as an example to other women who might want in future to do what I had done. It made the matter even more grievous that I had murdered an expatriate who had given ten years' unstinted service to the country, denying himself the pleasures of his homeland in the process. Nigeria would look like a primitive nation, and its people would be considered barbaric, if anything but the maximum penalty was laid on me.

The defence counsel did his best, arguing that I was an unfortunate woman whom society had denigrated and men had taken undue advantage of. My poor background was not my fault; we do not choose our parents. If I had been able to acquire a good, formal education, I would have led a proper life; I would not have been so dependent on men. John Smith had taken advantage of me, satisfying his sexual appetite with an elegant beauty queen, a thing to which his ugly features did not entitle him. And when it suited him, he had reverted to stereotypical racism, dumping his African mistress without ceremony. It was racism, colonial exploitation. No African would have done a similar thing. The African would have married both women and that would have been the end of the matter. But the hypocritical Scot wanted to eat his cake and have it. Besides, I had not meant to murder John Smith. It was an accident which might happen to anyone. A knife is thrown in anger, it meets its target, who falls and aggravates the wound. I was provoked and I only responded as any normal human being would. He went on and on. I should be discharged and acquitted.

In the end, the judge decided that I was guilty of the crime. He was an Englishman, Justice Dennis Brown, and may have been moved by the necessity to protect his kind. In any case, I wanted just one judgement: to be sentenced to death. I got my wish. I was to be hanged until I was dead, as an example to others.

I went back to prison hoping that they would carry out the sentence immediately. But nothing was going to happen as quickly as I wished it. The case would go on appeal, even against my will. The only thing that might help me was the fact that independence was very much around the corner. The departing British would not wish to leave my case up in the air. They would rather get it finished with – every British life was very important and must not be trifled with. So, the appeal got accelerated hearing and the sentence was confirmed. Again, I thought that it would be carried out with dispatch. But I was to learn that it had to go to the Governor-General, who had rights to exercise the prerogative of mercy and commute the sentence to life imprisonment or a pardon. The defence lawyer had applied to the Governor-General and I would again have to wait.

I waited in chains in prison but I was dead to the world. Even the world of the prison. Nothing mattered any more. My body was dead, so far as I knew. I could not feel pleasure, and I did not know pain. I lived, I ate to survive, my only pleasure that I did not have the courage to take my life. In any case, that would have been impossible in prison since we were well guarded. I hardly spoke to anyone, saying only a few words when it was absolutely necessary.

One night while I was waiting for final confirmation of the sentence, the Controller of Prisons turned up and himself removed my leg-cuffs. Then, motioning me to follow him, he led me to this same office where we are sealed now and gave me a dress in my size, taking away my prison uniform. He ordered me to wear the new clothes. I obeyed. Then he led me out of the prison.

There was a car waiting outside with a man in the driver's seat. The Controller of Prisons opened the door to the passenger seat and waved me into the car. Then he moved over to the driver, and I think I heard him say something about being back within the hour.

It was a very dark night and the streets were completely deserted. Familiar with the town as I was, I could not tell exactly where we were once we had left the precincts of the prison. The driver was silent throughout the journey. We arrived in front of a bungalow set in a large compound full of fruit trees, shrubs and hedges and the driver stopped the car, switched off the engine and made for the front door of the building. He opened the door, switched on the light in the room and then came to open the door of the car on my side. He invited me to get down, and taking me by the hand, led me into the house and on to the bedroom. As far as I could tell, there was no one else in the house.

The bedroom was dimly lit. On the dressing table were a number of bottles of alcoholic drinks, obviously put there for a special purpose. The man who had brought me, a huge fellow, broad-chested, black, mustachioed and well-dressed, poured drinks into two glasses and offered me one. I declined the offer. He drank up quickly, and started to undress, while he told me how he had fallen in love with me when he saw me in the magistrate's court. He wanted me for himself, no matter what happened. Now in the nude, he took my hand and began to caress me. I did not, could not, respond to him. That part of my life was dead. I had killed it long ago, the day I murdered John Smith. I said not a word as the man proceeded to undress me, lay me on the bed, and after a great fumbling effort, please himself. He might as well have been making love to a corpse. How he succeeded in deriving terminal excitement from this exercise I do not know. He eventually got dressed, urged me to do the same and then, planting a kiss on my cheeks, led me out again into the car and drove me back to the prison, where the Controller himself was waiting to receive me. I changed into my prison clothes and returned to my cell. It was not necessary for the Controller to ask my consent as he did not have to breathe a word of what had happened to anyone. This event repeated itself three or four times each month, over a period of three months.

Why did I not protest against this repetitive event? There was no need to: I was not participating in it. I was no longer alive, as I have said, and were I being led to my death instead of into a bedroom to be abused, for abuse it was, I would have behaved in exactly the same manner. It just did not matter. Nothing mattered any more. I was a mere stump of rotten wood, filled with stale milk.

Ah, but in the denouement, it did matter. When the papers for my execution arrived, the doctor came round to examine me. And it was found that I was pregnant. There was no way I could be hanged while I was in that state.

I did not know how to react to all this. Was I to jubilate? Was some trick being played on me again, by fate? I had always, like every woman, wanted a child. I had not even taken precautions against pregnancy. And yet, I had not, in spite of my numerous affairs, ever been impregnated. Now, here I was, virtually on the gallows, and after the abuse of my person, with child. I took it stoically and bore the pregnancy in a calm frame of mind.

As the months passed and my body changed, I began to nurse hopes for the future. For the child certainly, though not for myself. Would it be a boy or a girl? How would it grow up? Who would take care of it? What future would it have? Would it find the luck that I never had? What would fate have decreed for it? What fate was it that decreed that this child should be borne by a mother such as I, and conceived in such circumstances? Would the child ever know these facts? And if it did, what effect would they have on it? Would that child ever be grateful to its parents? To the world? Would it be a happy part of its society?

And I also wondered who would be taking care of the baby. Would it have to grow up in the prison with me? I did not have anyone in the whole world to send it to. So what would happen? These were questions to which I could not find an answer, and I shoved all my doubts aside. I had no one to discuss them with. Well, I suppose I could have asked the prison officers. But I had made up my mind not to speak until I was spoken to, and even then to keep my answers to monosyllables. Therefore, I kept my doubts to myself. No matter, I did occasionally have that delight which, I suppose, every woman has, in bringing forth new life. As the child kicked me in the stomach, I had a certain sensation, at once painful and pleasant. On such occasions, I thought of the man who had fathered the child. I did not even know him, his name, his profession or anything. Nor did I ever ask the Controller of Prisons, he who used his power to set up the game. After I was found to be pregnant, however, the game stopped. I did not see the Controller again and I did not get to meet his partner either. They just disappeared from my life. Well, it did not matter. I would have the child and take care of it, as far as was possible.

This last residue of life within me surprised me a bit. My frame of mind might have encouraged me to get rid of the child. To throw it away, whatever. The fact that I was thinking of taking care of it – was that indicative of a new attitude, borne of the fact that I was giving birth to a new life? Was I no longer dead to the world? Well, I'd see after the baby was born. The most important thing for the moment was to remain in good health and bear the child peacefully.

This duly happened. One early morning, I had labour pains and the night of that same day, my daughter was born in the prison infirmary. A healthy child she was, and to my eyes, pretty. I felt happy as I held the little girl in my lap. Yes, I was happy, even though it was for just one moment or so. And I was proud too – because I had successfully fulfilled one role assigned to women. This one great assignment is only allowed to women. No man can ever do it. It mattered a great deal to me, to all women, to the world, to society, to humanity. A grave responsibility, indeed.

I was reminded that day of the Ogoni folk-tale which explains why men do not get pregnant. Lewa, being pregnant, was treated cruelly by her husband, Lenee, who would often beat her and ask her to fetch and carry for him. Although she was pregnant, she still had to go to the farm, fetch water, cook for her husband and provide for his pleasure at night. He would bully her if she did not perform any of these tasks properly or on time.

Lewa, angry at his brutality, went to consult the oracle. She wanted the pregnancy transferred to her husband so that he would understand what it meant to be pregnant. The oracle, after questioning her, duly counselled her.

'Go home,' the oracle said. 'Be sure you share the bed with your husband tonight. Whatever he does, do not be angry with him. If he treats you badly again tonight, then your prayer will be answered.'

Lewa had travelled a long distance to the oracle and returned home late. Lenee was already fretting by the time she got back home. He berated her, wanting to know how she expected him to find food to eat and water to bathe in. Lewa was all sweet reasonableness and apologized to him. She prepared his dinner and served him and made the water hot for his bath. He complained about the quality of the food and the temperature of the water. Lewa apologized to him.

Later that night, they went to bed. At first, her husband would not allow her into the bedroom, just to show his displeasure over her behaviour that day. But she again apologized to him and he was mollified. They lay together in bed, and Lewa soon slept, so tired was she. Her husband would not let her be. He needed her, he said. She pleaded with him to wait until morning when she would have all the strength in the world to make love. He finally agreed to this, and fell asleep beside her.

The next morning, Lewa was the first to wake up. She found herself quite light and spritely. Her stomach was flat. Her pregnancy had disappeared; she stepped out of the room with light steps, a smile on her face. Later, Lenee woke up. He found it was not so easy to rouse himself from bed. What ... what had happened? His stomach protruded. He received a kick in the stomach. Oh! And he felt like throwing up. It was an uncomfortable, and unusual, feeling.

Then it occurred to him that he was pregnant. Pregnant? A man, pregnant? He called to his wife, Lewa. And she came to him smiling, her stomach all flat.

'I don't understand what's happening,' he moaned. 'I went to bed a man and now I wake up to find I am pregnant.'

'Ah. Wake up, man. Get up, it's morning. And time to get to the farm, but before that, prepare me my breakfast. And before that, let me have a hot-water bath. Keep the house clean, I don't like dirt around.'

The poor man was aghast. What would he tell his friends? How could he explain what had happened? He lifted himself slowly out of bed. No, he would not carry a pregnancy. He had to consult the oracle. And he went thither. On the way, he sang thus:

Zan lelenle zan Lewa
Zan lelenle zan Lewa oh zan!
Had her pregnancy
Zan lelenle zan Lewa oh zan!
Transferred to me
Zan lelenle zan Lewa oh zan!

He laid his complaint before the oracle, and sought what to do.

'You have been cruel to your wife,' the oracle said.

'Ah!' moaned Lenee.

'When a woman is pregnant, you have to be kind to her. You should care more for her then than when she is not pregnant.'

'Ah!' groaned Lenee.

'You will have noticed that in your present state, you are not as quick to take advantage as when you did not bear an additional load.'

'No doubt, no doubt.'

'I will transfer the pregnancy back to your wife. But you must promise me that henceforth, you will treat her courteously and politely.'

'I promise, I promise. I promise a thousand times.'

'Go home then, and keep your promise,' the oracle ordered.

Lenee returned home. When he got there late in the evening, his wife had his dinner prepared, his bath ready, and she was very solicitous of his comfort.

'Thank you, my dear,' he said as they lay in bed.

The following morning, Lenee had lost his pregnancy and Lewa was once again pregnant. But from that day, Lenee was all light and sweetness to Lewa. He no longer beat her, nor did he bully her.

And that is why men do not get pregnant. Had Lenee not obeyed the oracle, he would surely have got pregnant again and he would have been at the receiving end of the long stick. This story teaches us to be kind to pregnant women.

Later that night, the woman who had helped deliver me of my daughter came to me and said she would have to take the baby away.

'Where to?' I asked.

'Her father wants her. He's an important man. His child, he says, cannot grow up in a prison.'

'No!' I cried. 'I won't let go of my child.'

'Be reasonable. What can the child find here? How can you take care of her? Send her away where she will be happy. You will be doing her and yourself a favour.'

'Let me think about it,' I pleaded.

'We don't have much time. We have to send her away before sunrise.'

Left alone with my child, I cuddled her lovingly and wept tears I had not shed in a long time. And I spoke to her. 'Child, may you be lucky in your life. May your star shine as mine never did. Be protected from the evils of the world. May you find the education I never had, and men who will value you for what you are. May no man ever take advantage of you. God bless you, my baby. And may He grant that I see you again.' In the hope that I would meet her one day, I gave her a cruel, painful mark on the tenderest part of her body I could think of. That way, if I ever saw her again, I would always recognize her.

The baby cried and yelled in pain. I soothed her as best I could and when the woman came back, I asked for the Controller of Prisons. He came along, and I made him promise that he would take care of my baby and let me know wherever she was sent to. He promised solemnly, and I handed over my child in a bundle to him.

My heart bled as she was taken away, but deep inside me, a voice assured me that I would see her again before my death. The thought of my little girl was to sustain me through the many years of my imprisonment.

CHAPTER NINE

I was to spend twenty further years in prison. And every day of those years was like the next. In time, my sentence was changed to life imprisonment because, after independence, views of my behaviour altered, and it was thought that the sentence I had received was too harsh. I don't know by what process this happened but I was informed that there was a lot of argument on the pages of newspapers, and several pleas went to the authorities.

It mattered to me in only a little way: the thought that I might see my daughter again. I kept on wondering from day to day, from year to year, what she would look like, what she was doing. Where she was. And every year, on the anniversary of her birth, I recalled the prayer I had said for her the day she was born and taken away: 'May your star shine as mine never did.'

Every morning when I woke up and the doors were unbarred, I looked up at the iridescent clouds of sunrise and prayed for my daughter. When the key turned in the lock in the evening, I looked through the bars, searching for the shining stars and asking which was mine and which my daughter's.

Each day I hoped that she would come calling, and I'd get an invitation to the reception desk to receive the surprise of my life. Then as the years passed, I began to despair of this. I had been foolish to expect that I'd ever see the girl again. Where had they taken her after she left my arms that night? Were they able to find a mother who could give her milk? How could I be sure that the baby was in the hands of her father? Were there not enough women, unable to bear children, who were ready to kidnap babies? And who was a better baby to kidnap than mine, whose mother was a convicted murderess and could never look for her, whose father was unknown and would probably never be known? He might even deny having ever had anything to do with me, and there was no way I could prove it.

I also asked myself what constituted motherhood. The fact that I had had intercourse with a man and my egg had met with his sperm to produce a foetus? The care I took of this foetus during the mine months it stayed in me? Was it the blinding pain of the moment of birth which only a mother could ever know, even if it was forgotten the moment it was over? Or was it the care one took bringing up the child after birth until it became a man or woman capable of looking after itself and reproducing its kind? Which of these qualified one to call oneself a mother? What if, having grown up in the care of another, the girl whom I called my own should tell me that she does not know me and that I cannot be her mother? For all I knew, she probably bore no resemblance to me at all. All I would know her by would be the mark I gave her the day she was born. And that could easily have healed. So what claim to motherhood would I have?

Examining these questions, candidly, I would at times come to the conclusion that I was not a mother in the proper sense of the word, since all I had done was to bring the child into the world, and not by any wish of mine, but by a strange concatenation of circumstances.

But how could I be sure that if the girl heard my story, the full story of all that had happened, she would not pi.y me? That she would not accept that I had been buffeted by fate, prevented from performing duties which I would gladly have carried out? The story would therefore remain my prized possession. I would not tell it to anyone whatsoever. So far, no one knew it all. The lawyers in court had tried to piece the facts together and make a story, but they had failed. The story would only be told to the child of my womb, whenever she turned up, as I sometimes felt sure that she would. My desire would be to narrate all to her, sparing nothing whatsoever, so that she could decide if I was as evil as I had been made to look, or even as I thought myself to be. It would be for her to determine whether she would believe me or not. I had to have faith in that bond between mother and child, developed over nine months in the womb, which would always make us one, no matter what disagreements we had. When the eventual choice had to be made, child would always vote for mother, stand by mother.

So that in telling my story to my daughter, and apologizing for my neglect of her, I would win her forgiveness. I would tell her everything as it had happened.

I went over the story several times myself. And it fell into neat little episodes: my childhood, my time at school, my stay with the Manas, the return to Dukana and the death of Mother, Mama Bomboy and then Maybel, Donatus Adoga and John Smith. Neat pattern. As though it had been carefully laid out by some designer, with one waiting to take the baton from the other. Yes, I was the mere baton. And that was my problem, wasn't it? Everything was happening to me. I did not happen to anything or to anyone. Each time I tried to happen, disaster resulted.

But, come to look at it, how many people did happen to others? How many? As far as I know it, there were few. Mana happened to me. Yes? But suppose I had not been there, could he have happened? He brought me from my mother's and so it could be argued that he happened to me. He did not fish me out himself. He told his problem to the school headmaster, who came looking for me. So that in a sense, the happening was a question of an encounter between people, with the more powerful or the more advantaged prevailing. Good resulted if the more powerful prevailed positively and vice versa. But who controlled that positive or negative prevalence? That was what the world was about. There was just so much happening that no one was in control and no matter who had happened to me, I had to remember that I too had happened to others.

Lemona. My name. Happy encounter. Lucky encounter. Encounters made stories. Without encounters, there are no stories. Happy encounters are fairy tales. How had my mother given me such a name? Was she merely expressing a wish, a hope, for me? Or was she describing what had happened to her? Because for all I knew, the man who had happened to her did not bring her luck. Or was the luck her having had a child at all? But the way I had turned out, was that luck? Encounters lead to questions. There were just too many questions surrounding me.

The thoughts of a prisoner are many. The prison itself is a world of its own. Many things go on there, and I might even have led a life there if I had so wanted. But I had forsworn life itself and not even the thought of my child would change that. I ought to explain that. That my hopes for the child did not mean that I changed my attitude to the world. It only meant that deep within me, there was something bolted up, something which was meant for me alone and which remained so no matter what else was happening outside. It made me more introspective than ever before. And may have given certain signals about me to others. Not that I cared. What anyone thought about me did not matter. Nothing mattered.

Every day in prison was like the next. Many thoughts came knocking on the door of my mind asking to be allowed in, made comfortable and accepted as a part of me so as to help ease my boredom, the pain of repetitive inaction. Thoughts of beauty. I was thought to be an extraordinary beauty, right? Different from all the others. My mirror told me so, I cannot deny it. And I became convinced of it, after hearing it from so many people. But what had it brought me? What? The lust of men and one woman. None of them really cared for me. They cared for the image they had planted in their brains. The image was not me. Yet that was what drove them to say they wanted me. Me, not the image of me they had found. They were not being honest to themselves or to me. And I was too inexperienced to know. And they may not have known either.

No, but was that being fair to the likes of Edoo? He had really, really loved me, not so? Well, not quite. The fact that he had been a regular at my house for over six months before we even so much as held hands was not necessarily a mark of devotion. He could just as well have been playing his cards right. Hurry might scare me. And he needed this great beauty for his own satisfaction, his own ego. He satisfied himself, but died in the attempt. Maybe he was happier? Was he? How could I say? He was ever so fond of life. How did I know that Adoga would sort him out as he sorted me out? Adoga was even lenient with me, by comparison with what he did to Edoo. If Edoo had known that the encounter with me would lead to his death, would he have sought me? Would he? If I had known that my encounter with John Smith would land me in jail, send me to the gallows, would I have embraced the encounter? The man who took away all my belongings, all he had given me and what I had even got for myself, but left me with my life, was he not better than he who gave me more than I ever had in life but then led me to my present misery? Donatus and John, which was the better of the two? Time passes slowly in prison. The mind turns over a myriad of ideas, most of them useless. The sheer tedium forces you to go over your life, to examine and re-examine the missed opportunities, the ifs that would have made a difference had they not happened. If they had not happened. If. If you had not happened to someone or someone had not happened to you. If, if, if. A cruel world indeed. Who can claim to be happy in it? Adoga, for certain. Rising to the top of his company, assured of his family – his wife and happy children – a beautiful mistress waiting on his pleasure, money in his pocket. What else could he want? Public esteem? He also had that. But who would ever know of the beating Edoo handed to him? Each time he thought of that drubbing, he would be diminished in his own eyes. The thought that he had also been responsible for the man's death would haunt him. Or would it? Possibly not. And the way he had treated me. He'd certainly have a twinge of conscience the odd moment. But no one else would know that. Those who saw him from a distance might well envy him, thinking him a success. They would never know the many encounters which compound to sap his life, to reduce him to the common condition of humanity, even before death rings its final, common bell. Maybel might have been the envy of many a woman. She had all the creative comforts, led an independent life, the sort of life most women hankered after. But did they know the other side of her? That she had an appetite different from other women's? Did they? And did it not worry her that she would not bear children like other women did? And what of the girls she went after who were repulsed by her uncommon appetite? She really happened to me! After that first night, how I scrubbed my lips and all those parts of me she had rubbed herself against! But I could not bring myself to tell her how much I hated that part of her. She really regarded herself as the rival of my boyfriends, those ones who gave me at least some pleasure. How she must have suffered when I left her. And whatever became of her thereafter? Surprising I never got to meet her again. Our paths never did cross even though we were still in the same small town. What could she be doing now? She must have heard of my troubles. Yet they did not matter to her. Who knew to whom she was now happening? Or had someone happened to her? She had all those beautiful clothes. Did clothes attract men to women? If they did, and attracted the men she met, then they would find out that she did not care for them. Or they might not. And they would keep going after her, to plumb the depth of her mystery. And they might never be wiser, unless the likes of Uche, Ngozi and myself decided to demystify her for them. Then, would they hate her? Pity her? Laugh at her? What? Ah, nature was really capricious. Or should I say, cruel? Life is contrary. Wasn't it John who once told me that for every woman there is a man? And for every man a woman? A very tall, huge man finds comfort and happiness in a small, petite woman. Yet custom would dictate that he should have found a woman his size. But such a woman never happened to him until after he got hooked to the small woman and they both became the butt of jokes, a point of gossip, of wonder. Prison life is tedious, one long day stretching into another long day while life outside goes on, passing you by. You are the flotsam floating on water while in the depths fishes swim, feed, spawn, bite a bait and end up in a cooking pot. Mama Bomboy. The best person that ever happened to me. She died while I was still at Maybel's. I often called on her in those days, just to hear her talk. I continued to do my hair in her shed in the market and she would look at me, pity in her eyes, pity she constantly kept away from me. Did she know something I did not know? Could she have guessed how I would end up – in prison for the rest of my life? Why do angels like her die quickly? Young? I wonder what happened to her children? Particularly the two lissom girls? They would happen to some men some day. Or some men would happen to them. And there would result stories. Life is a series of stories, some exciting, others dull. Exciting and dull stories together make our world. Some get a lot out of the world. Others nothing at all. For yet others the world just happens to them, squeezing all out of them. Mother for instance, wherever she might be now. Why had my sentence been commuted to life imprisonment? Who was it out there who cared about me to torture me this much? I'd have been happier dead, joining John Smith, Edoo, Mama Bomboy and all those others who died every day but whom I did not know.

For some reason I did not know, I was moved from Port Harcourt prison to the maximum-security prison in Lagos. And I was there when the civil war broke out. I knew because of some men who got locked up there for some reason. I never asked what was happening to me or to others. I did not have to tell my story to anyone. And I did not want to hear any other person's story. Many must have wondered why I was like that. That was their business, not mine.

Long after the war ended, I got moved again, back to Port Harcourt prison. As the tedious days, months and years passed, I got a sense of the changes that were happening outside. Always from the gossip of prisoners. But it did not matter to me. At some moments, thoughts of my darling child would come coursing through my brain. Only then did I feel some slight sense of joy that I was still alive. Would she ever walk through the iron gate of the prison and come asking for me? Would she? Yes, she would. She would. Something tells me so. I see her in my dreams. She will come calling to hear my story. And that story will be a long story too. She needs to hear it. How I wish that the Controller of Prisons, who knows so much about us all, could suddenly turn up! But he never does. He has disappeared, walked out of my life. Is he dead? Will he remember the promise he made me to keep an eye on my daughter and to make her happy? Will he? Will he keep her in the dark about the story of her birth? I hope to God he does because I'm the only person entitled to tell her the story. Time burns slowly, each day like the next, in prison. And it will be thus until I drop dead, even if I live to be one hundred? What cruelty? What a life! Would it not be better just to take my life and end the torture? End the everlasting days and nights? Then my daughter would not have heard the story, the authentic story. But is she alive? What if she is dead? What then? No, she could not be dead. God takes care of His own. The thoughts run through my brain interminably, as I sit here, staring into space, having lost count of the days, months, year, divisions which do not matter at all to me in my condition. How boring, how tedious!

Then, one day, straight out of the blue, the news came. I was to be released. Why? To mark the twentieth anniversary of Nigeria's independence. I had been in jail for twenty-two years. The thought of going into the world outside of the prison frightened me. What would I go out to do? I was no longer young. I had nothing on earth, nowhere to go. The prison was safer for me. There was food, albeit unfit for human consumption. But I had endured it for twenty-two years, and it did not appear to have taken any toll on me. Physically, I was in good shape. But where would I go? Dukana? Stay in Port Harcourt? Oh, why did I have to face so many difficulties, so many insuperable obstacles? But the girl, my daughter. Yes, she was certainly one hope, beckoning me to get out of prison. I had to find her, wherever she might be. Even if she was dead, the knowledge would be enough. I was curious to know, whatever might have happened to her. I just had to know! And that was what sent me out of the prison yard in a tolerable frame of mind.

CHAPTER TEN

The forces at play in my wretched life were very much at work on that same day. Or should I rather say that my decision to keep to myself throughout my imprisonment ensured that I did not have information as to whatever was happening or was due to happen to me? Maybe if I had asked I would have been told who sent the clothes I was to wear as I left the prison yard? But I did not ask, and I suppose the prison staff were so fed up with my silence over the years that they no longer volunteered information of my affairs. Some may even have thought that I had gone mad. I am sure they whispered it to themselves.

New clothes were waiting for me at the reception desk. The Controller of Prisons himself lent me his office and I changed there. When I was done, he was on hand to wish me good luck and to see me out to the front gate. Believe it or not, there was a car waiting for me, to my utter surprise. I had not seen that make of car, the Morris Minor being the reigning car when I went to prison. But this was plush, elegant and very comfortable. The chauffeur opened the rear door for me and I settled into the car and was driven off.

The streets of Port Harcourt through which we passed were, I noticed, extremely busy. There were different brands of cars and buses about, and in great numbers too. This was a very far cry from the sleepy town I had left behind. It took me quite some time to recover from the daze I was in. I did not bother to ask the chauffeur any questions whatever. I chose to digest all that I saw on my own.

We soon got to a new residential estate, which had certainly not been there twenty years earlier. The car drew to a halt in front of a lovely bungalow surrounded by a bush and fronted by a green garden planted with shrubs and fruit trees. At the sound of the car, someone who appeared to be a steward stepped out, opened the car door for me and ushered me into the house. The car drove off. I walked into the lounge of the house.

It was well appointed, I observed, as I sat on one of the many settees in the extra-large room. There were none of those signs of family habitation which normally adorn houses, such as photographs and other artefacts. There were only paintings on the wall and plastic flowers in two vases on opposite corners of the room. I did not find a radiogram, which I expected to see in such a house. The steward moved towards a contraption that was on a small table opposite me and touched a button. In less than a minute, pictures appeared on the contraption and a voice began to speak.

'Madam wants something to drink?' the steward asked after a while. I declined the offer. I was not thinking of drinks. My mind was riveted on the fact that I was going to find it extremely difficult to settle into a new life, so much had things changed. I might even find it quite impossible to live in the changed circumstances.

The steward offered to show me my room and I followed him into another large airy room in which there was a large bed, dressed properly with cotton sheets. The view gave on to the lawn. I found some more clothes in the wardrobe. The steward explained that his master had instructed him to let me know that the clothes were mine. I thanked him. He asked when I would like to have lunch. 'One o'clock,' I replied. As he left the room, I asked what the time was. I had no watch. 'A little past ten o'clock,' he replied.

There was a cushioned chair in the room and I sank into it, lost in thought. Prison habits were still with me. I found my new surroundings quite strange. I suppose I should have asked the steward who his master was. But that did not occur to me at the time. The one thing I thought about was my daughter. Was she alive? Where could she be? Was it possible that she was living in town? She would have been about twenty years old at that time. Quite a young lady already, I thought. I was still thinking about her when I heard a knock on the bedroom door. I went to open the door and the steward I had seen earlier announced that lunch was served.

I lunched alone, thoughts of my daughter keeping me company.

It was a very delicious meal, but I did not have the appetite for it. After I had nibbled at it, much as a mouse before a tasty morsel of food, I retired to the room and lay in the bed. I soon fell asleep. And in my sleep, I had a dream in which I saw a young child, a girl who, laughing, beckoned me to play with her in an open playground. She had been part of a group of children but had left the group when she saw me. I followed her, but she kept backing away from me, past the other children. She was still laughing as she swiftly backed off, her eyes fixed on me. Yet I followed her, increasing my pace. Then we got to the end of the playground, beyond which was a gaping hole. It looked as though the child was going to fall into it. I could see it, but she could not. I shouted 'Stop! Stop!!' at the top of my voice as I increased my pace in order to catch up with her. As I drew level with her and stretched forward my hand to save her from falling over the edge, she smoothly metamorphosed into an old woman, thin and ugly with bulging eyes and great claws as fingers. The monster grabbed me by the hand and went for my throat, choking me. Frightened to death by the ogre, I yelled and screamed, and was still hollering when I opened my eyes to a knock on the bedroom door.

Dazed and confused, I sat up. I thought I was still in the prison yard and wondered why my immediate surroundings looked so strange. Another knock on the door brought me back to reality. I answered the knock and the steward informed me that 'Master' would like to see me. I answered that I would join him in a while. I took off to the adjoining bathroom and, for the first time in a long, long time, saw my reflection in the mirror. I was shocked by the sight. The years had taken their toll on my face. No, not just the years – grief, anxiety, boredom, distress, despair – name all the ill graces. There were stress lines, my skin was all dry, my hands crinkled and my face all drawn. My cheeks were also hollow. In short, I had aged even beyond my forty-seven odd years. I wondered, though, why I was shocked. After all, what had I expected? That I would still be the beautiful young woman of twenty-five or thereabouts who had been taken into custody and then condemned to death twenty-two years gone? I pulled myself together, washed my face, cleaned up and went to meet 'Master'.

He was a man of medium height, with a bulging paunch and flowing beard. Decked out in flowing white robes made of exquisite material, he wore a black, embroidered cap on his head. He wore a diamond signet ring on the middle finger of his left hand and exuded a certain opulence. But there was something sinister in his long square jaws, in his drooping eyelids. As I entered, he dropped the newspapers and stood up, extending to me his right hand, which I took.

'Lemma, you are welcome back to the world,' he said with a warm smile. 'Please sit down, sit down. God be praised. Amen.'

I sat opposite him, on the far side of the room. I did not recognize him at all, and must have shown my perplexity on my face. He put me at my ease immediately.

'I know you do not recognize me,' he said straight away. 'Many years have passed and I have changed, although you have not changed at all. I congratulate you on your looks. I thought that I would find a different person. But no, you are still beautiful, very beautiful. God be praised. I think you still remember the man who was Controller of Prisons when you had your daughter?' he asked, and paused to assess the effect of this communication on me.

I stared at him but could make no connection whatsoever. For one, the Controller of Prisons I knew was always in uniform and would have been quite trim. For another, I never did look properly at the Controller in question. All I had ever done was to obey any order he gave and on that night of the delivery, hand over my child to him.

'I can see that you do not remember at all. I am the one. My name is Chief Albert Chuku. I am the one to whom you handed over your daughter.'

My heart fluttered wildly. I had not known a smile for well on twenty-two years and could not make one now, although I was as happy as Punch. Here was luck. A slight movement of my lips, the light in my eyes, would have been the only indication of my joy.

'By the by, I think you are comfortable here?'

I indicated that I was by a nod of my head.

'This is my guest-house. I have just finished it. You are the first person to stay in it. If there is anything wrong, tell the steward and we will try to correct it.'

I stared steadily at him.

'Yes, I took part in the game leading to the birth of your daughter. My own reason was to help a friend. I knew that what I was doing was not correct. Either under the regulations of the prison service or under God. But I don't know whether I should give you my apology or give thanks to God. After all, it was that game which saved your life. Of course I did not know that my action would give such a wonderful result. However, we thank God that it turned out that way. God be praised.'

He paused again and looked to see if I was awake or asleep. I had been sitting so still, waiting anxiously for his news, the only important part of his news, that I thought he had cause to be anxious as to my alertness or otherwise.

'Life is like that,' he resumed. 'We do not know what will be the result of our actions. So, sometimes we make mistakes. But you know what our people used to say: every mistake in London is a style in Lagos. That is like what happened to me. As a result of that little game we played, there was an inquiry after they found out that you were pregnant. So I gave evidence at the inquiry. Of course I was guilty, no question about it. What I had to do was to stop other staff from being punished because of what I had done. So I was dismissed. No pension, no gratuity after twenty-four years' service. I was not happy at all. Well, never mind. I thought that my friend would help me to find something to do. To my greatest surprise, the man did nothing at all. He kept giving me different answers when I spoke to him. Even though he was the one who made me lose my job. You do not know your friends until you get into trouble. God be praised! I regretted all the things I did for him. You know how I introduced him to the most beautiful woman in the town when he was dying, just to touch her hand. I made it possible for him to meet her and then even God blessed him. A man who had no child before. As soon as he met the beautiful woman, it was like magic. She carried it for him. I even arranged to take the child from the mother and give it to him. How many other men would have done that for a friend? Yet when I got into trouble the man pretended that he didn't know me. He wouldn't even lift one finger, let alone one hand, to help me. But he did not know that God is good. I think, as they say, when He shuts one door, He opens a window. If I had not been dismissed from that prison job, if I had not lost my gratuity and pension, do you think I would have set up my own business? Look at me today. My own oil-servicing company, contracting company and estate business. God be praised! But wickedness should be punished so that people do not continue to practise wickedness. The world should be a better place!'

Albert Chuku appeared lost in the maze of his own thoughts. His monologue appeared to be addressed to no one in particular. I was silent, equally lost in thoughts of my daughter. I hoped that he would get back to that topic but I was not going to hurry him into it. I had waited for years to get the information. I could wait for another day, if it would take that long for Albert Chuku to get to that part of his story. The bitterness in his voice was unmistakable and complemented his sinister looks.

'I'm happy that I was able to welcome you from the prison. I know how it is after you have been there for so long. Adjusting to the outside world is not easy. You need help, you need understanding. And since I was in a position to do it and, as far as I could see, you did not have any friends, I decided to help. I had to help. It was a duty ordered by God for a poor, helpless woman. God be praised! I knew that you would not have clothes to wear, a place to stay or food to eat. I am happy to have provided all. I followed what was happening to you with interest through all these years. That is how I knew you were about to be released. Of course, news of you was in the papers quite regularly. I'm sure that that man, the father of your child, was the one who did it. Selfish man. Anyway, he helped you. He is a very big man now.

'After we had our disagreement, I do not know what he did with the little girl. When I gave him the baby that early morning, he had already hired a woman who would take care of her. In fact, he came to the gate of the prison with her. And he had also rented a flat for the woman, the nanny. The baby would be happy. I actually went there once or twice to see them. And I was quite happy about the level of care lavished on the baby. One year later, he decided to move the child to his house. It was at that point that I lost contact. So if you ask me, I will tell you that I do not know where your daughter is. I know that is the one thing you would like to know. I am sorry to disappoint you. However, I know where the man lives. He is a very big man now, as I said. But you can see him and ask him all the questions you want to. Do you want to meet him?'

I nodded the affirmative.

'I will make the arrangements,' he said. 'It will take me about one week to get everything ready. It is not so much the journey itself, but I have to clear my own desk. So, if you don't mind, spend the week getting used to the ways of the world once again. A car will be at your disposal and I'll send some money to enable you to buy anything you wish. I hope the arrangement suits you.'

'Thank you very much. It's most kind of you to do so much for me.'

'Never mind. You know the saying, "Man is God to man." I help you now, somebody helped me yesterday, you will help someone tomorrow. That is how life goes.'

'We happen to one another. With diverse results,' I thought to myself. Would that at long last I would happen positively to someone, even if that someone was my daughter! I was pleased to know that she did survive the first year of her life. I hoped and prayed fervently that she would still be alive and that I would finally set my eyes on her! What satisfaction that would surely give me! What joy, what fulfilment!

I had a week to wait for that possibility. Albert Chuku, true to his word, had sent a car and some money. But none of that was needed. I did not intend to step out of doors, and as I had a change of clothes, I considered myself well provided for, for the moment. Mr Chuku had obviously failed to appreciate the effect of a long imprisonment on me. Little did he realize how frightened (I'm sure that's the right word) I was. Even there in his parlour were changes to the world I had left behind. When I was taken into custody, there had been no television, for instance. Most lounges then had 'radiograms'. But now there were all sorts of strange gadgets in his guest-house with names I was yet to find out. I had found the television so fascinating that I had, in spite of myself, to ask the steward what it was. And that was the only question I hoped I would ever ask anyone. Evidently, Mr Chuku had, in his days as Controller of Prisons, known how to take care of prisoners when they were in prison. He would not have bothered to find out how his charges got on once they were discharged. He had asked me to 'get used to the ways of the world once again'. And that was easier said than done. It would have required quite some tutoring, I'm sure. Twenty-two years! And twenty of them had seen great changes in the country. A lot of my acquaintances would have either died or changed locations. For a moment, people like Maybel, Uche and Ngozi crossed my mind. But then, none of them had ever come to see me either in the period prior to my trial, or afterwards. The point was always my near-total isolation. My world had always been a small one – a few associates and no family as such. I had cut myself off from the village of my birth, Dukana, from its inhabitants, its ways. I was, in that sense, merely floating in the world, much like a water-weed, I dare say. My years in jail had reinforced that grimly, particularly as, of my own volition, I had remained closed within myself, like a clam. If I had to be brought out of my hard shell, I would have had, like a clam, to be boiled in water or had my shell forced open by other processes. Someone would have had to happen to me. It was not something I could do myself.

Now that I look back on it, I feel sure that Albert Chuku was probably well aware of all that and laid his plan accordingly. Yes, I'm sure he also knew as fact that I was in a very vulnerable position. As others had done, he decided to take advantage of me. But of that, more later.

I spent the week in Chief Chuku's guest flat holed up for most of the time in my bedroom. I went out of the bedroom only at mealtimes. Once, I did get out of the house and into the surrounding quarter to look at the shrubs, fruit trees and flowers. And it was a totally new experience.

Out there in the open air, I felt slightly lost. The sight of birds flying freely from tree to tree, chirping, twittering, whistling, reminded me forcibly of the loss of my freedom for half my life. When I saw a butterfly fluttering in brilliant colours from flower to flower, I was reminded of those days when I, well dressed, the cynosure of all eyes, flitted from party to party, from nightclubs to bars and restaurants. And it reinforced my sense of loss and added to the feeling of 'aloneness' which bore down heavily upon me. I dared not repeat the experience. I found that my freedom needed to be 'got used to'. And I recoiled from it in that week. I had only to hope that if I found my daughter, I might find hope, and if she was up to it, she might gradually win me back to life. If, on the other hand, I did not find her or, if finding her, she could not relate to me (and this second was very possible), then I thought I might go mad.

I thought I still had full control of my faculties, although I did wonder from time to time if those who came in contact with me and saw how I had withdrawn from all possible intercourse, including mere conversation with them, might not have thought otherwise. But it did not matter what they thought. My life did not matter to others. After all, I might as well have been dead, and society would not have cared, nor would it have made a difference to the world. Nor to three or four people. Or any other person, come to face it. I had to remember that even in my own wretched life, only four deaths had affected me: Mother, Mama Bomboy, Edoo and John Smith. And yet, how many people had died to my knowledge in the time between the deaths of Mother and John? No, one life is insignificant to society, to the world, unless that life has succeeded in making a difference to other lives and its absence portends a loss to men in the mass. Then would it be mourned. That was a right conferred on a very select few. This thought, or knowledge, reinforced my rejection of myself, and of the world and my place in it.

The week of waiting came to a merciful, if slow, end. Albert Chuku duly showed up at his company guest-house and informed me that he was ready to travel with me to meet the father of my child. I was ready on the instant. In my anxiety, I did not even bother to take a change of clothes. He had to remind me to do so, thrusting into my hand a small travelling bag. He had been told, no doubt, that I had not gone out of the premises in the week of his absence. He appeared tense, and his visage appeared as sinister as before. I recalled that he had not smiled either at our first meeting or now.

We drove in his car through much traffic out of town. He said we would be flying to Lagos, and I still remembered where the airport was. But once we drove out of town, I began to wonder what was happening. My doubts were later cleared. A new airport had been constructed and it was from there we were going to take off.

The airport itself was full of activity, with several would-be travellers waiting for the aircraft, which had not yet arrived. When it finally came, there was quite a scramble for seats. Chuku and I eventually struggled into seats in a plane in which all the seats were taken. It was all so different from the days before I went to jail. The pace was much more leisurely at that time and the travellers very few indeed, mostly expatriates. Now our own people were in control of their lives and they were enjoying a lot of things which were not within their grasp in the days before I was taken in.

The day had started on a bright note, with the sun casting its golden rays to all corners of the earth. I had seen that much even in the closely curtained room where I had slept. The sun, not to be kept out, had crept through the space between curtain and door and bade me answer its greetings. In the afternoon as we drove to the airport, the sun came shimmering down, but the car was air-conditioned, again a new experience for me, since the cars I rode in my time in the free world had nothing of the sort. I kept telling myself how much things had changed.

As the plane taxied off, there was no indication whatsoever of the turbulence that was to come. I had never in my life flown and were I in a position to be excited, I would have felt that sensation. But most of me was dead, and I did not experience fear either. Life, for me, meant seeing my daughter and it was to that I bent all my hopes and prayers. The possibility that it might soon happen was the only meaning to my existence and if I died after setting my eyes on her, I would die happy.

I sat next to Albert Chuku. Realizing my frame of mind, he did not attempt to make conversation with me and for the first thirty minutes or so, the flight was uneventful. Seated next to the window, I was able to look down at the clouds below and wonder at this marvellous invention of man. The pilot had informed us that the flight would last an hour or thereabouts.

Then the voice came over the loudspeaker system asking us to fasten our seat-belts, as rough weather was expected as we commenced our descent to Lagos. The pilot had hardly finished speaking when the plane began to lurch from side to side like a ship on a troubled sea. Anon, the plane suddenly went down, losing height without warning and throwing unwary hostesses off their feet. A cry of distress issued forth from the lips of passengers. Still the plane was not done. It rattled and shivered, rose up and went down, and gave signs that it might crash. I looked through the window and observed the dark clouds all about us. Outside, it was raining, and a sudden burst of thunder seemed about to split the plane. I could hear some call the name of Jesus several times. I felt like throwing up. Albert Chuku, obviously an experienced flyer, bid me take hold of myself, assuring me that we were not in danger as such. The most dangerous part of any flight was at take-off and landing, and no matter how stormy the weather in mid-flight, the plane was not likely to crash.

We soon arrived over Lagos and here the pilot advised that owing to adverse conditions on the ground, we would not be able to land immediately. He would have to circle the Lagos air-space for a while until he got advice from traffic control to land. We circled for what seemed like hours while my heart beat a wild tattoo. The meeting with my daughter was being unduly delayed. Ah, but I had waited twenty-two years and more. Another hour or two would scarcely make that much of a difference, surely.

We finally touched down in pouring rain and grateful passengers tumbled out of the plane and found their way to the arrival hall. I walked closely behind Albert Chuku, sloshing through the puddles of water on the tarmac as the rain beat me mercilessly. At the arrival hall, there were two men waiting for us and they led us to a waiting car outside. Albert and I sat at the rear while the two men sat in front, one of them at the steering wheel. We drove off.

We made progress slowly as the rain had created a flood on the roads and several cars, unable to move through the flood, came to a stop and had to be parked on the side by their unfortunate drivers. The rain came down relentlessly, covering the windscreen as the wipers laboured in vain. And the heavens flashed lightning and rumbled thunder. Albert Chuku leaned over to me and asked me not to worry. We would soon get to our destination. The father of my child, he said, was a Supreme Court judge and living in well-quartered premises. But there would be no problem my getting in to see him. Although he was not a trustworthy man, he had no doubt at all that I would be able to see him. From all he knew, he thought I would be well received by him; the only person I had cause to worry about, if at all, was his wife, a cruel woman if ever there was one, who had no child of her own and was a thorn in the side of her husband. Leastways, I would be able to get information about my daughter and we would take up the matter from there. When we got to the judge's house, Chuku would not go in with me because his differences with the judge were deep-seated and had lingered for a long time. He was, he said, doing me a favour because he felt responsible for what had transpired between me and the judge at the time he was the Controller of Prisons. He understood perfectly the way I felt about my daughter and hoped that I would do everything, everything, to gain access to her.

There was a lull in the rainfall, but the wind continued to blow, giving notice that the thunderstorm was not about to stop. We inched forward gradually. It was not yet night, but everywhere was pitch dark. The headlights picked out houses, shrouded in mystery. This was totally unfamiliar territory and I did not attempt to find out where we were. Albert Chuku continually looked at his watch as if he was working against the clock.

We drove for over an hour through that dreadful thunderstorm until we arrived in a well-laid-out suburb with beautiful houses in surrounding gardens. The car came to a stop before one of those houses. Chuku appeared quite familiar with the area. He looked at his watch again, got down from the car, spoke to the guards at the gate and then invited me to alight from the car.

'I'll be waiting for you here,' he said. 'Don't be long. I wish you luck.'

The gates of the compound opened and I passed through and walked with rather uncertain steps towards the house. It was a fairly long walk, in the rain, the house being set far from the gate. The thought did not cross my mind that I had taken too many things for granted. Suppose I should come to some harm where I was going? And then, I thought, what harm could ever come to me again? After all, did my life matter any? Hadn't I longed for death which refused to come? In any case, my daughter was the most important thing and whatever I went through to see her . . . But what if she refused to accept me because I had not really been a mother to her – well, there was no point to all that now. I stood before the carved front door of the opulent building. I rang the doorbell and waited. The rain continued to pour down and the wind lashed about noisily, driving the rain in my direction. I waited for about two minutes and then rang again. Still there was no answer. I looked back in case the guards at the gate might be coming to tell me that there was no one at home. That was most unnecessary; if there had been no one at home, the guards would have said so from the very beginning. There had to be someone at home. I rang the bell again. Then I heard a shuffling of feet behind the door and a turning of the key in the lock. The door opened and a shrill voice said, 'Come in.'

I stepped indoors and the door shut behind me. The man who opened and shut the door had trembling hands. And he was greatly emaciated. In pyjamas, with a dressing gown draped around him, he succeeded in giving the impression that he was a mere bag of bones. He wheezed a few words which sounded like 'sit down, sit down' and shuffled towards the lounge from the reception area.

'Excuse me,' he wheezed, 'I can't see you properly. I have to get my spectacles from the study.'

He shuffled into an adjoining room. While he did that, I took a look round the room. It was magnificently decorated. The hand of a woman was surely there in the flowers meticulously arranged, in the curtains which matched the floor carpet. Photographs adorned the walls; the wedding photographs of two young, happy people, the man in a judge's robes, the woman in a lawyer's wig and gown. There were no pictures of children, nor of one child. If this man was the father of my daughter, he evidently did not hold her dear, or the child was not welcome in the house.

I say 'if the man was the father of my daughter' because I did not recognize in the man who stood before me the individual who had spent those nights outside of the prison in a private house with me twenty years or so earlier. It is true that I had not observed him closely at that time, being mentally dead to all that was going on. But it is also equally true that that man, if I recall well, was healthy, robust and elegant, so different from this frail asthmatic with a wheezing voice shuffling around now.

He soon returned, his spectacles on his nose.

'Did you have an appointment with my wife? I don't recall having given anyone an appointment for this evening,' he said as he took a seat opposite me.

'No, I don't have an appointment,' I said.

'Who are you,' he wheezed.

'I'm Lemona,' I replied simply and looked him squarely in the eyes. I could see instant recognition in his eyes, and at the same time, hints of consternation.

'Lemona. Yes, yes. You're out now. Thank God. I played my part in your release. I had to. Yes, I had to. Thank God. But hold on, let me see if Elsie's in.'

He pressed an electric bell near where he sat and waited a while. Might Elsie be his daughter? My heart pounded away. When no one answered, he excused himself and climbed the marble stairs to the rooms on the upper floor. I heard him knock on the door and wheeze 'Elsie, Elsie!' Receiving no answer, he came back into the lounge. At that same moment, the doorbell rang and he shuffled towards the door and opened it. 'Elsie,' he wheezed. 'You've been out?'

Elsie, a large woman in a shirt and blouse, and with a wig on her head, came in. Her eyes darted past him towards me as though she expected me to be there.

'Who's that over there?' she asked, the hostility in her voice quite unmistakable.

The frail, asthmatic man was tongue-tied. He stood rooted to the spot near the door, which remained half open, letting in a gust of wind.

The large woman moved swiftly towards me and peered at me, hissed, and went back to the man. Towering above him, she let forth in a voice of scorn and contempt, 'You had to bring her to complete my disgrace, didn't you? It's not enough, the tricks you played to get the murderess out of deserved jail, where God knows, she ought to have served her life sentence so society might be rid of vermin of her sort. You got her out using your blasted influence and then not one week after, she's here in my parlour discussing with you behind my back. What haven't you done to me, Bamidele? What haven't you done? You deprived me of the pride of a woman, you made me live without a child to comfort me while you went out to enjoy yourself, fulfil yourself as a man, bringing a bastard to my house, and you were not man enough to tell me the truth. And you supposed that I, Elsie, true daughter of my father, would never find you out. The advantages you men take of women! You thought me a fool, didn't you? I'd never find out. I did, Judge. I could well have handed you over to the law, criminal that you are, but I forbore from it for old times' sake. And you promised me, false man that you are, that we'd put it all behind us. You thought I didn't know all you did to save that murderess from the fate that was truly hers? You thought I didn't know! I was saving my anger for this final moment, because I expected you to give me this last insult – disenchanting my home with a murderess. No, don't say a word. Not a word. You had it coming to you all your life and I'm going to give it to you. You deserve to die!'

I saw the man shrink and tremble, his jaws clattering uncontrollably, his legs collapsing spastically beneath him so that by the time the woman rained blows on him, he was all but dead. The blows finished him off and he fell in a heap on the floor, the back of his head hitting the step of the staircase and blood spurting out like water from a spigot.

Then the large woman turned on me. I had already stood up as she pummelled her husband. Now she rushed at me with a 'You slut, murderess, I'll teach you to ruin a decent home. One murder was not enough for you. You had to commit more!' She rushed at me and hit me hard. The blow forced me instantly to my knees. Then she bore down on me, raining blows on my head. I was stunned. I had not, in all my life, ever fought anyone. In the face of such provocation, I mustered sufficient strength in my kneeling position to sweep her by the legs off her feet. She landed on the floor with a thud and I leapt at her and held her by the throat. My arms and hands were like steel as I banged her head several times on the floor, and she choked and moaned until life oozed out of her. I did not relax my hold until she was dead.

I got up and stood there panting as through the door walked two men, one of them in plain clothes – he had been in the car with me and Albert Chuku – the other in police uniform. They looked over the scene. The policeman put cuffs on my wrists while the man in mufti made a telephone call. When I was eventually led away, Albert Chuku was nowhere in sight.

The case this time did not take much judging. I was a psychopath. Having murdered my lover twenty-two years earlier, I returned upon release to wreak revenge on the magistrate who had done the preliminary investigation into my first murder and committed me into prison custody. My behaviour in prison confirmed my predilections. I had maintained a studied silence, which made me something of a nutcase. The fact that I had also murdered the judge's wife, who had come into the house just as I completed the murder of her husband, showed that I was extremely dangerous and merciless. I was duly condemned to be hanged by the neck until I was dead.

I did not dispute anything that was said. I refused to disclose all that had happened even though my counsel quizzed me endlessly. I did inform him that Albert Chuku had brought me to Lagos and led me to the judge's house. But I would not say who Albert Chuku was, nor would I speak of the relationship he had with the murdered judge. Somewhere at the back of my mind though, was the realization that Albert Chuku had set me up. That would have explained the presence of the plain-clothes man at the airport and the disappearance of Albert Chuku after the incident. I also suspected that the week between my release and the date of our travel had been spent preparing the ground for the event. Whether he had links with the judge's wife I could only guess. But none of that mattered. My life had run its wretched course and all I had to do was to wait for that death for which I had longed ever since John Smith died.

I was subsequently transferred from Lagos to Port Harcourt to be hanged in the town where I had spent most of my life. And so, tomorrow morning, the story which you have just heard will come to an end. I don't know that there is anything to judge in it and I am not asking for understanding either. I accept all that has happened. I am not even sad that I could not influence any of the events in any way at all. I seem to have been like seaweed floating upon the tide. But aren't we all like that? Who really controls or influences what happens to them? If I have any regret at all, it's only that I did not get to see that child of my womb. And yet even up to last night, I did not give up hope. But even if I saw her, would I give up hope? And now, my question to you. Why did you come to hear my story?

CHAPTER ELEVEN

It was already the early hours of the morning. I had listened for over sixteen hours to the story which Lemona had to tell. And it had begun to dawn on me that I had not been asked to see her just for the fun of it. The narration had pointed out the fact that I appeared in the story not merely as the daughter of my murdered father. Could Lemona have been my natural mother? This question nagged at me without end. There was a missing link. I begged leave to ask but one question, and she consented to answer it.

'The child you bore, what mark did you leave on her by which you hoped to identify her in the course of time?'

'I bit off the tip of her left finger, the smallest finger, Heaven forgive me,' she replied.

I held my hands together beneath the table. Lemona was my natural mother! But if so, and since I looked so very much like my father, why had she not recognized me! Or had she? She had not observed him closely when first they met on those earlier occasions before I was conceived. And on the day of his death, he had grown much older and was a frail asthmatic. Should I show her my left hand and tell her the murdered judge was my father? That she was my mother? But was I sure she was my mother? If I told her that she was my mother, would it help her? Might she not want to hear my own story all over? Did I really feel for her as a mother or was I merely touched as any listener to her story might be? In the end, I decided not to tell her about my father and my finger. And when she again demanded why I had come to her, I merely said it was a part of my academic studies. And I thanked her for the trouble she had taken to narrate her story to me.

She stood up and embraced me warmly. There were tears in her eyes as she said goodbye. And my tears flowed freely as I watched her move out of the room.

The Controller of Prisons had remained in an adjoining room

and when he judged that we had finished, he came to lead Lemona back to her cell. He rejoined me in his office thereafter. He had to let me out of the prison.

'You had a long chat with Lemona,' he said.

'It wasn't a chat. She was telling me her life,' I replied.

'A real story she must have had to tell.'

'Yes. An extraordinary story.'

'I should love to hear it myself.'

'Not tonight, surely. I'll retell it in a book. And dedicate it to you. I'll send you a copy. Without you, I might never have heard such an extraordinary story.'

'She'll be hanged at six o'clock – in four hours or so.'

'Alas!' And the tears poured down my cheeks.

The car which had brought me was waiting outside the prison gate. The driver had gone to sleep. I roused him, got into it and, waving the Controller of Prisons goodbye, drove off.

I arrived at my temporary residence to find the steward waiting for me. He had worried himself stiff for my sake. He asked if I would like something to eat. I had not the appetite. I retired to bed and lay there wide-eyed, counting the hours until it was six o'clock. At which time I said prayers for the repose of Lemona's soul. It was just as well I did not know how people are hanged, but several scenarios passed before my eyes in any case. And always I saw that beautiful form, that pretty face hanging by the neck, dangling lifeless in some nearby room. It was too much to bear and I wept copiously. I was still shedding tears when sleep mercifully delivered me from my anguish.

A tap on my bedroom door woke me up many hours later. I looked at my watch. It was three o'clock in the afternoon. I had been sleeping for seven or eight hours and was very hungry. The steward it was who had come knocking. Did I care for lunch? I did. I had a bath, dressed and sat at the dining table, and nibbled at the food before me. I had just finished my coffee when my host and his wife, Mr and Mrs Dabibi, came in.

'Hello, Ola,' Mr Dabibi greeted me. 'Good afternoon.'

'Good afternoon, sir,' I replied, and curtseyed to them.

'You're having a late lunch,' Mrs Dabibi said.

'My first meal since breakfast yesterday.'

'Ah. You spent a long time in the prison, I dare say,' Mr Dabibi said.

'Yes.'

'And did you see Lemona?' Mrs Dabibi asked.

'I did. We spent over fourteen hours together. She told me the story of her life. A touching story if ever there was one.'

'I expect so. I saw her twice at Port Harcourt Club. When she was with her lover, John Smith. A beautiful young woman. A pity she's ended this way.'

'She was hanged at six o'clock this morning,' I said, as the tears rained down my cheeks. I held my head in my hands.

Mrs Dabibi came to me and wrapped her arms round me.

'Cheer up, Ola, cheer up. Wipe your tears. I don't know what you heard yesterday. And I do not know enough of the hanged woman. But every death diminishes each one of us. When love becomes a cause of death of whatever kind, both men and women lose. For life itself is love. And what would we be if love died?'

I calmed down by degrees and Mr Dabibi apologized to me for having had to travel when first I arrived in Port Harcourt. He was aware, he said, that I didn't know him well enough, if at all. But he had been a close friend of my father. Their friendship had lasted over twenty-five years and he was not surprised that he had been made the executor of his will. He could say that he knew everything about Justice Kole Bamidele, including the strained relationship with his wife, Elsie, except that he had a daughter, Ola, who was studying in the United States. Yet shortly before his death, he had asked him to get in touch with her and invite her home at her leisure. 'I knew that he had an interest in the Lemona case,' Mrs Dabibi said, 'but I had presumed that interest to be purely professional. He often told me that she did not deserve to die but I had attributed that to the great admiration he had for beautiful women, beautiful things. However, his request that I make it possible for Lemona and Ola to meet surprised me. And when later he was murdered by the same Lemona, I was intrigued.

'I confess I am still intrigued by it all. Perhaps you, Ola, will be able to educate me on all this, clear my doubts. You have seen

Lemona. Although you have not met your father, there is a letter here which he charged me to give you. After you've read the letter, we'll have a clear picture, no doubt. His wish was that you should read the letter before I revealed the contents of his will to you. We'll leave you to read the letter and then we'll meet at dinner time.' And he gave me a sealed letter.

'I know this is a difficult time for you,' Mrs Dabibi said, 'but you know you have friends here. I am a woman and you can share confidences with me. I'm at home all afternoon should you need me. Cheer up now, child.'

'Thank you, so very much. I'll for ever be obliged to you for your kindness to me.'

'Don't mention it,' Mr Dabibi said as he and his wife left me alone.

I went into my bedroom and broke the seal of the envelope and read the letter from my father. Dated a week before his death, it read thus:

My Darling Ola,

I am feeling poorly these days and my end is probably near. I think it necessary in these circumstances to write to you, to explain a few things to you, to ask forgiveness of you, if thus I may win your love and understanding, both of which I have probably lost in these years when you neither saw me nor heard from me. I trust that the mitigating circumstances will soften your heart towards a lonely, weak, old man buffeted by fate and fortune, though respected by men.

My wife Elsie and I met as young students at the University of Edinburgh. There were only five Africans in the entire university and Elsie was the only woman. As we both came from Nigeria, we became friends. We were not just friends, we fell in love the moment we met, and I do not think that there was any doubt in our minds as the years passed that we would become man and wife. We shared the same interests and we both wanted to become lawyers and we did go to the Inns of Court in London together and qualified the same day. Elsie was two years older than me but it did not matter in the least to me at the time. In our final year at Edinburgh, Elsie became pregnant and she suggested that we get married. I was not averse to marriage to her but we would not be able to support a child as students. Elsie did not want an abortion; she wanted to bear the child. I insisted on an abortion and to assure her that a child was not the only thing that could keep us together, we got married in the registry office. Thereafter, she had the abortion, although all her instincts, as she told me, were against it.

That abortion was to lead to my eventual ruin and it may yet cause me my death. For, years later, we were to find that Elsie's womb had been damaged in the course of the operation and that she would never be able to bear children. Elsie never forgave me for insisting on the abortion and held me for ever responsible for any and every problem she had in life. She nagged me at every turn. I became a hen-pecked husband, harried in my own house and finding comfort everywhere else but in my marital home. The worst came out of her if she suspected that I had smiled at another woman, looked at another woman, spoken to another woman. That would mean that I was proposing to have a child of my own, whereas I had made it impossible for her to fulfil herself as a woman.

The situation in my home was intolerable. Be that as it may, I loved Elsie with all my heart. I had always loved her and I was quite content to be childless if only that would assuage her. I did feel guilty about her childlessness, but I would have been happy if she had not been so paranoid about it. I suggested that we adopt a child but Elsie would not hear of it. Instead, she chose to patronize the churches, traditional healers, anything and anyone that promised even the possibility of her becoming pregnant again.

Things were as well as they could be until we got transferred to Port Harcourt. I had become a magistrate at this time and Elsie a state counsel. We were doing well as far as our careers were concerned. I had looked forward to the Port Harcourt posting because I knew that John Smith, a Scot and a friend from our undergraduate days at the University of Edinburgh, was there. John had developed a love of Africa through his association with me and Elsie. We had lost touch a while after our return to Nigeria but I had run into him at Lagos airport when he was on his way home on annual leave. He had spoken to me of the enchanting African beauty he had fallen in love with in Port Harcourt and I was desirous of meeting both of them and renewing acquaintances.

Imagine my shock when on assumption of duty at Port Harcourt, the first case I was assigned to was a preliminary investigation into the murder of John Smith by his African lover! I did my duty under the law but I could never get out of my mind the beautiful young woman who had committed the murder. The fact that the murdered man was white and that Nigeria was still a British colony added a new dimension to the case, as did the fact that the accused was too shell-shocked, too traumatized by the death of her lover. I recalled distinctly the endearing terms in which John spoke of Lemona, for that was her name, and of her love for him. And I felt deep in my heart that the death could only have happened by accident. However, there was nothing I could do. Based on the evidence before me, Lemona's case was taken to court, and I followed the case until she was condemned to death.

I knew that the racial nature of the murder would send Lemona to an early death and that no appeals would succeed in reprieving her. In the circumstances – and I confess here to my weakness, but plead mitigation – I decided on the only course of action which would save her from the gallows. She had to be pregnant.

The decision was strictly mine and I accept full responsibility for it. I had struck up a particular friendship with Albert Chuku, a man on the rise who was at that time Controller of Prisons and had full charge of Port Harcourt prison, where Lemona was held. We often met at the golf club and I told him how I had fallen in love with Lemona and that I thought the only way of stopping her being hanged was to make her pregnant. Could he made arrangements for me to meet with her clandestinely?

Albert was totally unwilling to do so initially. He answered that it would be placing his job at risk and that in any case, I could not be sure that mating with Lemona would produce the desired pregnancy. I argued that fear of failure should not stop me from making the attempt. Albert would not give way. How was I sure that the woman would go along with me? The argument went on for months. Eventually, I gave Albert my assurance that should he lose his job as a result of the arrangement I was forcing on him, I would ensure that he did well in private business, which was burgeoning at the time, with the oil industry getting established in Port

Harcourt. I had certain contacts, I assured him, which would radically transform his financial standing.

Hesitant to the very end, Albert finally gave way to my entreaties and I met with Lemona on several occasions over a period of time. I cannot state in all honesty that she was a willing participant. Indeed, I noticed a remarkable resignation about her, as though her body was not a part of her and that I could do anything I wished with that which she had rejected. To my absolute surprise, and delight, she did become pregnant. And you, Ola, were the result of that union. Lemona was saved from the gallows when the time came and she was found to be pregnant. I had succeeded in my design.

I took my beloved daughter away from the prison and her mother because I was not going to allow her to grow up in such a dreary atmosphere. I made suitable arrangements for a nurse and found a flat, which I rented specifically for the purpose. And I often spent a lot of my spare time there. All this was kept rigorously from Elsie, who continued to pester me and make my home an absolute misery.

But more trouble was in store for me. The prison authorities instituted an inquiry into the Lemona affair and at the end of it, Albert Chuku was dismissed from his position. He protected me throughout the inquiry, not mentioning who he knew to be the seducer of Lemona. He became upon dismissal my direct responsibility, asking me to fulfil the promises I had made to him. I took care of him immediately, ensuring that he did not suffer any loss of salary and renting him the sort of accommodation he was used to while I made inquiries through my contacts for a new business career in the oil industry for him. I was fairly well off, having inherited substantial property from my parents in Lagos and taking care of Albert initially was no problem for me. Unfortunately for me, Albert was not willing to wait. Two years after his dismissal, he served me notice. If at the end of twelve months, I had not established him in business as I had promised, he would take steps to ensure that I did not live happily while he wallowed in misery.

The silver lining to the looming cloud on the horizon was my daughter, my Ola, who was growing up healthy and strong, a delight to me. I spent long hours with her, deriving much pleasure therefrom.

When eventually I ran out of the time Albert had stipulated, he did what I feared. He ratted on me, informing Elsie about all that had transpired between me and Lemona and about Ola and where I kept her.

All hell was let loose. This was what Elsie had been looking for all her life to prove my perfidy. And she had me cheap. For one, the fact that I was the magistrate who investigated Lemona's case and sent her into prison custody, only later to cavort with her, was bad enough. Then the criminal aspect of taking her surreptitiously out of the prison for my own pleasure. And then my deal with Albert Chuku. Whichever way the matter was looked at – professionally, morally, legally – I was at fault. And Elsie made sure that I did not forget it. A bright legal mind herself, I believe she set up a court to try me, found me guilty on all counts and sentenced me to eternal perdition. She reprieved me temporarily in order to hand down the punishment in little daily doses, much like medicine. Awake or asleep, at work or at play, Elsie poured scorn and contempt on me, made me feel unworthy even in my own eyes, and if I dared plead for forgiveness, threatened me with instant exposure, disbarment, imprisonment, eternal penury and total disgrace. She would show me that she was her father's daughter.

Hell hath no fury like a woman scorned, they say. If I had not believed that saying, if I had not understood it, Elsie was proof of it. And what could I do against her but ask for forgiveness – and remind her of the ties which bound us and had bound us from our undergraduate days, the love which I insisted and she well knew I still had for her. All of which incensed her the more and made her intensify her torture and torment of my person.

Albert had told her where you, my child, were living with the nurse. She went visiting and ticked off the nurse, letting her know the part she was playing in a crime and what would happen to her when the law finally caught up with her and her worthless employer. I wonder to this moment that she did not throttle my beloved child.

Fear of what she might do to you made me decide to take you to London, to the landlady in whose house I had stayed while I was a student at the Inns of Court. She gladly accepted you, to my greatest relief and joy, and having settled terms with her, I returned home in great heart. My intention was to spend my annual leave with you in London. However, the moment Elsie knew that I had sent you out of Port Harcourt, although she did not know precisely where I had sent you to, she made absolutely sure that she did not let me out of her sight on any of the holidays we took together. The days I spent with you in London were stolen by means that I do not care to repeat for my own self-respect. Let it be said, though, that I did care for and love you enough to ensure that I gave you those stolen moments. And you were a lovely child, made in your mother's image, as I was made in my mother's image. I left sufficient funds for you to get the best of a public-school education and was happy about it. For I knew that the best gift I could make you was a first-class education, apart from the parental care which I well knew even money could not buy. I could not, alas, provide the latter, so I made sure that the former was properly taken care of. I am happy that you justified the expense fully and made me even prouder as a father.

Let me confess, my dear daughter, that I did not give Lemona up. True, I have not set eyes on her since the last night we had together. But it was my aim that she should not remain in prison one day longer than was necessary. Accordingly, I used my contacts in the press to mount a campaign for her release. It was a most difficult task, took me a very long time and tested my patience besides. When it eventually happened, I was the happiest man in the world.

By then, I had risen quite high on the Bench, thanks to God. But my health had begun to deteriorate. I had also grown older, but no matter how old I grew, with Elsie too, she never forgave me my sins. Indeed, she formed an alliance with Albert Chuku so that between the two of them, I had enemies both inside and outside of my house. There was no way I could escape them. I could not divorce Elsie because she would have used that against me, and she would not divorce me because it suited her to have me under her cruel mercy, a very footstool for her pleasure.

As I write this letter, I know that your mother will soon be released from prison. I am of the view that you should meet with her and take care of her. Whatever she may have done, she has paid a heavy price for it, to society and to God. I do not know in what state of mind she is going to be, but whatever the case, I think it your responsibility to help heal her wounds. I know that having never known her, having not grown up in her care, you may not feel that she has been a mother to you. But I assert that she is your natural mother, and that bond of blood which binds mother and child certainly subsists between you. It is also possible that she will have been hankering after you – I do not know that it can be otherwise. If so, your meeting her should give her fulfilment and something to live for after so many years in prison.

As I say, I feel the hand of death upon me, although I cannot say how soon that event will be. I am sending this letter to my dear friend Opubo Dabibi, a worthy attorney who, in the event of my death, I have nominated as executor of my will. He is under instruction to give it to you sealed as it is, so that the communication in it will be strictly for your eyes only, and you are free to do whatever you please with it. In the event that on your mother's release from prison I am still alive, I will undertake to introduce you to each other and will resign from the Bench in order that we may find a life together, no matter what Elsie feels. For I owe you that duty and I would not be ashamed of Lemona's past because, I reiterate, she has paid society whatever debts she may have owed it.

And now, my dear Ola, my darling daughter, I am done. I ask your forgiveness for my neglect of you these many years. I hope that having explained the circumstances, you can find it in your heart to forgive me. I have made every arrangement for your comfort and hope that you will find in that additional testimony of my feelings for a daughter whom I love dearly and would gladly have given more.

May God in His abundant mercies bless and keep you. This prayer comes from a living father,

Kole Bamidele

I read and reread this letter several times, with mixed emotions. Added to the story I had heard from my mother, yes, my mother Lemona, yesterday, I was confused, distressed and depressed. I lay in bed, staring at the ceiling while myriad thoughts tugged at my heart, pulling me in contrary directions.

I declined the invitation to dinner with the Dabibis, pleading a headache and a loss of appetite. They understood and did not pressure me, leaving me to my thoughts. Nor did I sleep all night. My situation defied analysis, and no matter what I did, the images which appeared before me were not in the least edifying. Out of the darkness of that miserable night came the hoo-hoo of toads, the hoot of an owl, beeping bats swooping about my head, ghouls and ghosts walking about, and a lone black star expiring in a dark, clouded sky. My parents had happened to me, as my mother would have said, and left me at the mercy of the powerful forces of darkness. Would I ever escape them?

I sat at breakfast with the Dabibis the next morning, dry-eyed but still low in spirit. After breakfast, Mr Dabibi took me to his study and read me my father's will. He had left me all he had on earth. I was his sole heir and it amounted to quite a lot by Mr Dabibi's estimate.

'Sell it all, and give the proceeds to charity,' I instructed Mr Dabibi. He was completely flummoxed. 'No, my dear, you don't understand what you say.'

'I do, sir,' I replied calmly.

'All right. Let's say we'll think about it in another three months or so after you have had time to digest all the information you have received in the last two days. There's no reason to be hasty.'

'My mind's made up. I know what I want,' I affirmed.

'And that is?'

'An air ticket back to the United States to complete my studies.'

'Fair enough. And after that?'

'Time will tell. I dare not make any plans. Let's hope that some man does not happen to me and reduce me to the same level as the woman who bore me, or that other one my late father married.'

'Ah.' Mr Dabibi looked at me, askance.

'No, I'm not passing judgement. I'm merely praying.'

'Ah,' Mr Dabibi repeated. 'Shall we return to all this after three months? Are we agreed?'

'If you say so.'

'Good. I'm happy for my late friend, for you and for myself. I hope that we can do right by everyone when we've had time to take all the extenuating circumstances into consideration. Besides, your father ought to have a memorial to his name. He was a respected judge and a good friend.'

I winged my way back to my studies the following day. As I mounted the steps of the plane, I thought how unfair it is that children do not choose their parents.

READ MORE IN PENGUIN

In every corner of the world, on every subject under the sun, Penguin represents quality and variety – the very best in publishing today.

For complete information about books available from Penguin – including Puffins, Penguin Classics and Arkana – and how to order them, write to us at the appropriate address below. Please note that for copyright reasons the selection of books varies from country to country.

In the United Kingdom: Please write to *Dept. EP, Penguin Books Ltd, Bath Road, Harmondsworth, West Drayton, Middlesex UB7 0DA*

In the United States: Please write to *Consumer Sales, Penguin USA, P.O. Box 999, Dept. 17109, Bergenfield, New Jersey 07621-0120*. VISA and MasterCard holders call 1-800-253-6476 to order Penguin titles

In Canada: Please write to *Penguin Books Canada Ltd, 10 Alcorn Avenue, Suite 300, Toronto, Ontario M4V 3B2*

In Australia: Please write to *Penguin Books Australia Ltd, P.O. Box 257, Ringwood, Victoria 3134*

In New Zealand: Please write to *Penguin Books (NZ) Ltd, Private Bag 102902, North Shore Mail Centre, Auckland 10*

In India: Please write to *Penguin Books India Pvt Ltd, 706 Eros Apartments, 56 Nehru Place, New Delhi 110 019*

In the Netherlands: Please write to *Penguin Books Netherlands bv, Postbus 3507, NL-1001 AH Amsterdam*

In Germany: Please write to *Penguin Books Deutschland GmbH, Metzlerstrasse 26, 60594 Frankfurt am Main*

In Spain: Please write to *Penguin Books S. A., Bravo Murillo 19, 1° B, 28015 Madrid*

In Italy: Please write to *Penguin Italia s.r.l., Via Felice Casati 20, I–20124 Milano*

In France: Please write to *Penguin France S. A., 17 rue Lejeune, F–31000 Toulouse*

In Japan: Please write to *Penguin Books Japan, Ishikiribashi Building, 2–5–4, Suido, Bunkyo-ku, Tokyo 112*

In South Africa: Please write to *Longman Penguin Southern Africa (Pty) Ltd, Private Bag X08, Bertsham 2013*

READ MORE IN PENGUIN

INTERNATIONAL WRITERS – A SELECTION

The Stories of Eva Luna   Isabel Allende

'One could happily read more of these fantastic, sexy and sometimes macabre tales that treat the reader to Isabel Allende's extraordinary imagination' – *Guardian*

Perfume   Patrick Süskind

'Born in sweaty, fetid, eighteenth-century Paris, Grenouille is distinctive even in infancy. He has "the finest nose in Paris and no personal odour". With wit, a Gothic imagination and considerable originality, Süskind has developed this simple idea into a fantastic tale of murder and twisted eroticism controlled by a disgusted loathing of humanity ... Clever, stylish, absorbing and well worth reading' – *Literary Review*

Scandal   Shusaku Endo

'Spine-chilling, erotic, cruel ... it's very powerful' – *Sunday Telegraph*. '*Scandal* addresses the great questions of our age. How can we straddle the gulf between faith and modernity? How can humankind be so tender, and yet so cruel? Endo's superb novel offers only an unforgettable bafflement for an answer' – *Observer*

Love and Garbage   Ivan Klíma

The narrator of Ivan Klíma's novel has temporarily abandoned his work-in-progress – an essay on Kafka – and exchanged his writer's pen for the orange vest of a Prague road-sweeper. As he works, he meditates on Czechoslovakia, on Kafka, on life, on art and, obsessively, on his passionate and adulterous love affair with the sculptress Daria.

Katherine   Anchee Min

'The picture of China as a country that has lost all morality, thanks to Mao, is compelling ... the forces shaping the characters are brilliantly evoked' – *The Times Literary Supplement*. 'Remarkable not only for the light it sheds on recent Chinese history and for its portrayal of a passionate platonic female relationship, but also for its original and invigorating style' – *Sunday Telegraph*

READ MORE IN PENGUIN

INTERNATIONAL WRITERS – A SELECTION

Sleepwalker in a Fog Tatyana Tolstaya

'In her second volume of short stories Tatyana Tolstaya confirms her standing as a writer of major importance ... it is like roaming through a large house stuffed with secrets: you never quite know what you will find, but it's all there. No need to go outside' – *Independent on Sunday*

The Mambo Kings Play Songs of Love Oscar Hijuelos

'An exuberant portrait of the Hispanic music scene and Cuban family culture in New York in the forties and fifties ... One of the many glories of this beautifully sentimental novel is that its author writes about sex with an unashamedly florid Latin hand' – *The Times*

Half of Man is Woman Zhang Xianliang

'The gulag literature of the Soviet Union is world-famous, but China's equivalent is almost unknown. *Half of Man is Woman* is exceptional not only for belonging to this genre but also – in China – for daring to make sexuality its theme, together with politics, freedom and identity' – *Observer*

Dance Dance Dance Haruki Murakami

'Reading *Dance Dance Dance* is a bit like being taken blindfold on a joy-ride ... a bizarre tail-chase that deploys all the genre clichés of the hardboiled American thriller – beautiful, mysterious women, wisecracking detectives, paranoia, murder' – *Independent on Sunday*

Strange Pilgrims Gabriel García Márquez

The twelve stories in this collection by the Nobel prizewinner chronicle the surreal, haunting 'journeys' of Latin Americans in Europe. Linked by themes of displacement and exile, these vivid, magical tales of love, loneliness, death and the memories of past life conjure images of beauty and horror at once ethereal and exquisitely sensual.

READ MORE IN PENGUIN

INTERNATIONAL WRITERS – A SELECTION

Steppenwolf Hermann Hesse

This Faust-like and magical story of the humanization of a middle-aged misanthrope was described in *The New York Times* as 'a savage indictment of bourgeois society'. This self-portrait of a man who felt himself to be half-human and half-wolf can also be seen as a plea for rigorous self-examination and an indictment of intellectual hypocrisy.

The Labyrinth of Solitude Octavio Paz

Winner of the 1990 Nobel Prize for Literature, Mexican poet and essayist Octavio Paz is one of the world's foremost writers. 'A profound and original book ... with [Lowry's *Under the Volcano* and Einstein's *Que Viva Mexico!*] *The Labyrinth of Solitude* completes the trinity of masterworks about the spirit of modern Mexico' – *Sunday Times*

August 1914 Aleksandr Solzhenitsyn

Against a brilliantly evoked backcloth of Russian society *August 1914* follows the army as it advances into East Prussia to face catastrophic defeat at the hands of the Germans. 'Without doubt the greatest Russian novelist of this century' – *Sunday Times*

The General in His Labyrinth Gabriel García Márquez

'A lyrical description of an old man at the dusk of his life ... *The General in His Labyrinth* ... is also a portrait of Simón Bolívar, the extraordinary general who pushed the Spanish out of South America and whose dream of independence made him a hero in five countries ... the mixture is rich ... Sentence for sentence, there is hardly another writer in the world so generous with incidental pleasures' – *Independent*

Lenin's Brain Tilman Spengler

Dr Oskar Vogt has dedicated his life to the discovery of the scientific basis of human genius. Through scandals and a suicide, from the Great War to the 1930s, Vogt pursues his dream. He dissects the brains of animals and soldiers and is invited – bizarrely – to probe the brain of Lenin himself ...

READ MORE IN PENGUIN

A CHOICE OF FICTION

Simeon's Bride Alison G. Taylor

In the North Wales village of Salem, beauty and poverty, suspicion and superstition, walk hand in hand, and police and criminals know each other only too well. But nobody admits to knowing anything about the woman found hanged in the woods ...

The Afterlife and Other Stories John Updike

'Here we have an Updike afterlife of revisitings, uneasy remarryings, leave-takings, and stocktakings ... when he gets his hands on the short story the master can do no wrong' – *The New York Review of Books*

Signals of Distress Jim Crace

In the winter of 1836 the *Belle of Wilmington* is wrecked off Wherrytown. The Captain and his American sailors flirt, drink, brawl, repair the damage to their ship ... and inflict fresh damage on the town. Another visitor marooned far from home is Aymer Smith, a man brimming with good intentions both for the *Belle*'s black slave cook, Otto, and for himself, a virgin and a blunderer in search of a wife.

The Stories of Eva Luna Isabelle Allende

'Vibrant and colourful ... twenty-three magical tales, of anger that changes to laughter and revenge that turns into love' – *Literary Review*. 'Like a plate of hors-d'oeuvres, each one tempting, some as exquisite as caviare ... stunning' – *The New York Times Book Review*

Shards of Memory Ruth Prawer Jhabvala

The Master, an enigmatic spiritual leader, has an influence which spreads through four generations and across three continents. Elsa Kopf, a wealthy American, moves from New York to Hampstead to dedicate herself to the dissemination of the Master's message. Deserting her husband, Kavi, an Indian poet, she and her companion Cynthia take up the cause of the great man. 'Jhabvala weaves this dance of generations with economy and humour ... her gallery of characters is vividly realized' – *The Times*

READ MORE IN PENGUIN

A CHOICE OF FICTION

Grey Area Will Self

'A demon lover, a model village and office paraphernalia are springboards for Self's bizarre flights of fancy . . . his collection of short stories explores strange worlds which have mutated out of our own – *Financial Times*

A Frolic of His Own William Gaddis

'Everybody is suing somebody in *A Frolic of His Own* . . . Among the suits and counter-suits, judgements and appeals, the central character, Oscar Crease, scion of a distinguished legal family, is even suing himself for personal injury after his aptly named Sosumi car runs over him as he hot-wires the ignition . . . Like all satire this is a very funny but also a very serious book' – *Independent on Sunday*

The Children of Men P. D. James

'As taut, terrifying and ultimately convincing as anything in the dystopian genre. It is at once a piercing satire on our cosseted, faithless and trivially self-indulgent society and a most tender love story' – *Daily Mail*

The Only Problem Muriel Spark

Harvey Gotham had abandoned his beautiful wife Effie on the *autostrada* in Italy. Now, nearly a year later, ensconced in France where he is writing a monograph on the Book of Job, his solitude is interrupted by Effie's sister. Suddenly Harvey finds himself longing for the unpredictable pleasure's of Effie's company. But she has other ideas. 'One of this century's finest creators of the comic-metaphysical entertainment' – *The New York Times*

Small g: a Summer Idyll Patricia Highsmith

At the 'small g', a Zurich bar known for its not exclusively gay clientele, the lives of a small community are played out one summer. 'From the first page it is recognisably authentic Highsmith. Perhaps approaching her lesbian novel *Carol* in tenderness and theme, it has a serenity rarely found in Highsmith's world' – *Guardian*

BY THE SAME AUTHOR

A Month and a Day
A Detention Diary

With an Introduction by William Boyd

In May 1994, after the deaths of four moderate Ogoni elders, political activist and writer Ken Saro-Wiwa, together with eight others, was arrested for their murder. Following a show trial on 2 November 1995, he and his co-defendants were found guilty and sentenced to be hanged. Despite massive international publicity the executions were carried out on 10 November.

A Month and a Day is the extraordinary and moving account of Ken Saro-Wiwa's period of detention in 1993, and is also a personal history of the man who gave voice to the campaign for basic human and political rights for the Ogoni people. It was fear of his success that made Saro-Wiwa the target of the despotic Nigerian military regime. Arrested on 21 June 1993, ostensibly for his part in election-day disturbances, he describes in harrowing detail the conditions under which he was held. He writes of his involvement with the Ogoni cause and his instrumental role in the setting up of the Movement for the Survival of the Ogoni People (MOSOP).

Ken Saro-Wiwa was an outspoken critic of the Nigerian government – he accuses them of genocide – and of the international oil companies, notably Shell, which he holds responsible for the ecological destruction and terrible industrial pollution of his homelands. Yet, despite a brutal government campaign against the Ogoni, he always advocated peaceful and non-violent protest. Eventually Ken Saro-Wiwa was released as a result of intense international pressure, but in May 1994 he was arrested again and remained in prison until his death.